# DEBBIE MACOMBER

## CAN THIS BE CHRISTMAS?

MIRA®

ISBN 1-55166-455-0

CAN THIS BE CHRISTMAS?

Copyright © 1998 by Debbie Macomber.

**Printed in U.S.A.**

For my dear friend Betty and her Judge
Many years of happiness, my friend
To the new
Mr. and Mrs. Jim Roper

# *One*

*"I'll Be Home for Christmas"*

A robust version of "Little Drummer Boy" played in the background as Len Dawber glanced at his watch—for at least the tenth time in five minutes. He looked around the depot impatiently, hardly noticing the Christmas decorations on the windows and walls—the cardboard Santa's sleigh, the drooping garland and blinking lights.

Len was waiting with a herd of other holiday travelers to board the train that would take him to Boston. The snowstorm that had started last evening meant his early morning flight out of Bangor, Maine, had been canceled and the airport closed. Although the airlines couldn't be blamed for the weather, they'd done everything possible to arrange transportation out of Maine. Len suspected more than a few strings had been pulled to get seats on the already full mid-morning train. Maybe some of the original passengers canceled, he thought with faint hope.

Because, unfortunately, that crowded train was his only chance of making it to Boston in time to connect with his flight home for Christmas.

Len got to his feet, relinquishing his place on the hard station bench to a tired-looking man. He walked quickly to the door and stepped outside. He lifted his gaze toward the sky. Huge flakes of snow swirled in the wind, obscuring his view. His shoulder muscles tensed with frustration until he could no longer remain still. This was exactly what he'd feared would happen when he'd awakened that morning. Even then the clouds had been dark and ominous, threatening his plans and his dreams of a reunion with Amy.

Despite the snow that stung his eyes and dampened his hair, Len began to pace back and forth along the platform, peering down the tracks every few seconds. No train yet. Damn it! Stuck in New England on Christmas Eve.

This was supposed to be the season of joy, but there was little evidence of that in the faces around him. Most people were burdened with luggage and armfuls of Christmas packages. Some of the gift wrap was torn, the bows limp and tattered. The children, sensing their parents' anxiety, were cranky and restless. The younger ones whined and clung to their mothers.

Worry weighed on Len's heart. He *had* to catch the Boston flight, otherwise he wouldn't make it home to Rawhide, Texas, today. He'd miss his date with Amy and the family's Christmas Eve celebration. Part of his precious leave would be squandered because of the snowstorm.

There was another reason he yearned for home. Len didn't intend this to be an ordinary Christmas. No, this Christmas would be one of the best in his entire life. It had everything to do with Amy—and the engagement ring burning a hole in his uniform pocket.

Len had enlisted in the navy following high-school graduation and taken his submarine training in New London, Connecticut. Afterward, he'd been assigned to the sub base in Bangor, Maine. He thoroughly enjoyed life on the East Coast, so different from anything he'd known in Texas, and wondered if Amy would like it, too....

Len was proud to serve his country and seriously considered making the navy his career, but that decision depended on a number of things. Amy's answer, for one.

A real drawback of military life was this separation from his family. On his most recent trip home last September, he'd come to realize how much he loved Amy Brent. In the weeks since, he'd decided to ask her to marry him. They planned to be together that very night, Christmas Eve—the most wonderful night of the year. Once they were alone, away from family and friends, Len intended to propose.

He loved Amy; he had no doubts about that. He wasn't a man who gave his heart easily, and he'd made sure, in his own mind at least, that marriage was what he truly wanted. In the weeks since their last meeting, he'd come to see that loving her was for real and for always.

They hadn't talked about marriage, not the way some couples did, but he was confident she loved him, too. He paused for a moment and held in a sigh as the doubts came at him, thick as the falling snow. Lately Len had noticed that Amy seemed less like her normal self. They hadn't talked much, not with him saving to buy the diamond. And it was difficult for Amy to call him at the base. So they'd exchanged letters—light newsy letters with little mention of feelings. He had to admit he found their letters enjoyable to read—and even to write—and the cost of stamps was a lot more manageable than some of his phone bills had been. The truth was, he couldn't afford to spend money on long-distance calls anymore, not the way he had in previous months. His airfare home hadn't been cheap, either.

It wasn't as if he'd put off traveling until the last minute, which Amy seemed to suspect. He'd been on duty until the wee hours of this morning; he'd explained all that in a letter he'd mailed earlier in the week, when he'd sent her his flight information. Although Amy hadn't come right out and said it, he knew she'd been disappointed he couldn't arrive earlier, but that was navy life.

He hadn't received a letter from her in ten days, which was unusual. Then again, perhaps not. After all, they'd be seeing each other soon. Amy and his parents were scheduled to pick him up in Dallas, and together they'd drive home to Rawhide. He closed his eyes and pictured their reunion, hoping the mental image would help calm his jangled nerves. It did soothe him, but not for long.

He had to get home for Christmas. He just had to.

This was Cathy Norris's first Christmas without Ron, and she refused to spend it in Maine. She'd buried her husband of forty-one years that October; her grief hadn't even begun to abate. The thought of waking up Christmas morning without him had prompted her to accept her daughter's invitation. She'd be joining Madeline and her young family in Boston for the holidays.

Cathy had postponed the decision until last week for a number of reasons. To begin with, she wasn't a good traveler and tended to stay close to home. Ron, on the other hand, had adored adventure and loved trekking through the woods and camping and fishing with his friends. Cathy was more of a homebody. She'd never flown or taken the train by herself before—but then, she was learning, now, to do a great many unfamiliar things on her own. In the past Ron had always been with her, seeing to their tickets, their luggage and any unforeseen problems. He had been such a dear husband, so thoughtful and generous.

The battle with cancer had been waged for a year. Ron had put up a gallant fight, but in the end he'd been ready to die, far more ready than she was to let him go. Trivial as it seemed now, she realized that subconsciously she'd wanted him to live until after the holidays.

Naturally she'd never said anything. How could she, when such a request was purely selfish? It wasn't as if Ron could choose when he would die. Nevertheless, she'd clung to him emotionally far longer than she should have—until she'd painfully acknowledged that her fears were denying her husband a peaceful exit from life. Then with an agony that had all but crippled her, she'd kissed him one final time. Holding his limp hand between her own, she'd sat by his bedside, loving him with her entire being, and waited until he'd breathed his last.

Ron's death clouded what would otherwise have been her favorite month of the year. She found it devastating to be around others celebrating the season while she struggled to shake her all-consuming grief. She'd accepted Madeline's invitation as part of a concerted effort to survive the season of peace and goodwill.

Charting a new course for herself at this age was more of a challenge than she wanted. Life, however, had seen fit to make her a widow one month, then thrust her into the holiday season the next.

She was doing her best, trying to cope with her grief, finding the courage to smile now and again for her children's sake. They realized how difficult the holidays were for her of course, but her daughters were grieving, too.

This snowstorm had been an unwelcome hitch in her careful plans. Madeline had urged her to come sooner, but Cathy had foolishly resisted, not wanting to overstay her welcome. She'd agreed to visit until the twenty-seventh. Ron had always said that company, like fish, began to smell after three days.

''Mom,'' Madeline had said when she'd phoned early

that morning, "I heard on the news there's a huge snow-storm headed your way."

"I'm afraid it arrived last night." The wind had moaned audibly outside her window as she spoke.

"What are you going to do?" Madeline, her youngest, tended to worry; unfortunately she'd inherited that trait from her mother.

"Do?" Cathy repeated as if a fierce winter blizzard was of little concern. "I'm taking the train to Boston to join you, Brian and the children for Christmas. What else is there to do?"

"But how will you get to the station?"

Cathy had already worked that out. "I've phoned for a taxi."

"But, Mom—"

"I'm sure everything will be fine," Cathy said firmly, hoping she sounded confident even though she was an emotional wreck. She felt as though her life was caving in around her. Stuck in Bangor over Christmas, grieving for Ron—that would have been more than Cathy could handle. If spending the holiday with family meant taking her chances in the middle of a snowstorm, then so be it.

The first hurdle had been successfully breached. Listening to Andy Williams crooning a Christmas ballad, Cathy stood in line at the Bangor train depot, along with half the town, it seemed. The taxi fare had been exorbitant, but at least she was here, safe and sound. She'd packed light, leaving plenty of room in her suitcase for gifts for her two youngest granddaughters. Shopping had been a chore this year, so she'd decided simply to give Madeline and Brian a check and leave it at that, but she couldn't give money to her grandchildren. They were much too young for that. The best gifts she could think to bring them were books, plus a toy each.

Madeline had consented to let Lindsay and Angela, aged three and five, open their presents that evening following church services. Then the children could climb onto Cathy's lap and she'd read them to sleep. The thought of holding her grandchildren close helped ease the ache in her heart.

Everything would be all right now that she was at the depot, she reassured herself. Soon she'd be with her family. The train might be late, but it would get there eventually.

All her worries had been for nothing.


Matthew McHugh hated Christmas. And he didn't have a problem expressing that opinion. As for the season of good-will—what a laugh. Especially now, when he was stuck in an overcrowded train depot, waiting for the next train to Boston where he'd catch the flight into LAX. The timing of this snowstorm had been impeccable. Every seat in the station was taken, and people who weren't sitting nervously paced the confined area, waiting for the train, which was already fifteen minutes late. Some, like that guy in the navy uniform, were even prowling the platform—as though *that* would make the train come any faster.

Christmas Eve, and the airports, train depots and bus stations were jammed. Everyone was in a rush to get some-where, him included. As a sales rep for a Los Angeles-based software company, Matt was a seasoned traveler. And he figured anyone who spent a lot of time in airports would agree: Christmas was the worst. Crying babies, little old ladies, cranky kids—he'd endured it all. Most of it with ill grace.

His boss, Ruth Shroeder, who'd been promoted over him, had handed him this assignment early in the week. She'd purposely sent him to the other side of the country just so he'd know *she* was in charge. Rub his face in it, so to speak. This could easily have been a wasted trip; no one bought computer software three days before Christmas. Fortunately he'd outfoxed her and made the sale. By rights, he should be celebrating, but he experienced little satisfaction and no sense of triumph.

Ruth had been expecting him to make a fuss, demand that the assignment go to one of the junior sales reps. Matt had merely smiled and reached for the plane tickets. He'd sold the software, but was left feeling that although he'd won the battle, he was destined to lose the war.

And a whole lot more.

Pam, his wife of fifteen years, hadn't been the least bit understanding about this trip. If ever he'd needed her support it was now, but all she'd done was add to his burden. "Christmas, Matt? You're leaving three days before Christmas?"

What irritated him most was her complete and total lack of appreciation for his feelings. It wasn't like he'd *asked* for this trip or wanted to be away from the family. The fact that Pam had chosen the evening of his departure to start an argument revealed how little she recognized the stress he'd been under since the promotions were announced.

"I already said it couldn't be helped," he'd explained calmly as he packed his bag. His words were devoid of emotion, although plenty of it simmered just below the surface. He carefully placed an extra shirt in his bag.

Pam had gone strangely quiet.

"I'll be home Christmas Eve in time for dinner," he'd promised, not meeting her eyes. "My flight gets into LAX at four, so I'll be back here by six." He spoke briskly, reassuringly.

Silence.

"Come on, Pam, you have to know I don't like this any better than you do," he said, and forcefully jerked the zipper on his garment bag closed.

"You're going to miss Jimmy in the school play."

He was sorry about that, but there were worse things in life than not seeing his six-year-old son as an elf. "I've

...ked to him about it, and Jimmy understands.''

...his wife didn't.

...what was he supposed to say?'' Pam demanded.

Matt's shrug was philosophical.

"You were away when Rachel had the lead in the Sunday-school program, too.''

Matt frowned, trying to remember missing that. "Rachel was in a Sunday-school program?''

"Three years ago… I see you've already forgotten. It broke her heart, but I notice you've conveniently let it slip your mind.''

Matt had heard enough. He folded his garment bag over his arm and reached for his coat and briefcase.

"You don't have anything else to say?'' Pam cried as she stormed after him.

"So you can shovel more guilt at me? Do you want me to confess I'm a rotten father? Okay, fine.'' His voice gained volume. "Matthew McHugh is a rotten father.''

Pam blinked back tears. Matt longed to hold her, but they'd gone too far for that.

"You aren't a bad father,'' she said after a moment, and his heart softened. A fight now was the last thing either of them needed. He was about to tell her so when she continued. "It's as a husband that you've completely failed.''

Matt swore under his breath. Any tenderness he'd felt earlier shattered.

"You're leaving me to deal with Christmas, the shopping, dinners, everything. I can't take it anymore.''

"Take it?'' he shouted. "Do you know how many women would love to be able to stay home with their families? You have it easy compared to working mothers who're out there competing in a man's world. If you think shopping and cooking dinner is too much for you, then—''

Pam's expression grew mutinous. "My not working was a decision we made together! I can't believe you're throwing that in my face now. If you're saying you want me to get a job, fine, consider it done.''

Matt's fist tightened around his briefcase handle. That wasn't what he wanted, and Pam knew it.

"All I'm saying is I could use a little support.''

"It wouldn't hurt you to support me, either,'' she snapped.

They glared at each other, neither willing to give in.

"Have a good time,'' she said flippantly. "Just go. I'll do what I always do and make excuses for you with the children and your parents. I'll be at the school for Jimmy, so don't worry—not that you ever have.''

If Matt heard about this stupid Christmas pageant one more time, he'd blow a fuse. Rather than continue the argument, he headed out the door. "I'll call you in the morning.''

"Don't bother,'' she exploded, and slammed the door in his wake.

Matt had taken his wife at her word and hadn't phoned once in the past three days. It was the first time in fifteen years on the road that he hadn't called his family. Pam had the number of his hotel, and she hadn't made the effort to call him, either. They'd argued before, all couples did, but they'd never allowed a disagreement to go on this long.

Now as he stood in the crowded depot, waiting for the train to arrive, Matt was both tired and bored. For a man who'd purposely avoided any contact with his wife, he was in an all-fired hurry to get home.

This should be the happiest Christmas of Kelly Berry's life. After a ten-year struggle she and Nick were first-time parents. She liked to joke that her labor had lasted five years. That was how long they'd been on the adoption waiting list. Five years, two months and seventeen days, to be exact. Then the call had finally come, and twenty hours later they'd brought their daughter home from the hospital.

already talked to him about it, and Jimmy understands.''
Even if his wife didn't.

In less than a day, their entire existence had been turned upside down. After the long frustrating years of waiting, they were parents at last.

This would be their first trip home to Macon, Georgia, since they'd signed the adoption papers. Brittany Ann Berry's grandparents were eager to meet her.

The infant fussed in her arms and let loose with a piercing cry that cut into Neil Diamond's rendition of ''Jingle Bells.'' A businessman scowled at them; Nick, muttering under his breath, grabbed the diaper bag. Doing the best she could, Kelly gently placed the baby over her shoulder and rubbed her tiny back.

''She's all right,'' Kelly said, smiling to reassure her husband while he rummaged through the diaper bag in search of the pacifier.

As Nick sat upright, he dragged one hand down his face, already showing signs of stress. They hadn't so much as left the train depot and already their nerves were shot. Despite their eagerness to be parents, the adjustment was a difficult one. Nick had proved to be a nervous father. Kelly wasn't all that adept at parenthood herself. She smiled again at Nick, accepting the pacifier. Everything would be easier once Brittany slept through the night, she was sure of that.

Her two older sisters were much better at this mothering business than she was. Never had Kelly missed her family more; never had the need to talk out her fears and doubts been more pressing.

This flight home was an extravagance Nick and Kelly could ill afford. Then the storm had blown in, with all its complications, and they'd been rerouted to Boston by train.

A whistle sang from the distance, and the sound of it was as beautiful as church bells.

The train was coming, just like the man at the ticket counter had promised. She listened to the announcement listing the destinations between here and Boston as people stood and reached for their bags. Nick automatically started gathering the baby paraphernalia.

They were headed home, each and every one of them. A little snow wasn't going to stand in their way.

# *Two*

*"I Wonder as I Wander"*

The train filled up quickly, and Len was fortunate to find a seat next to a grandmotherly woman who pulled out her knitting the moment she'd made herself comfortable. Mesmerized, he watched her fingers expertly weave the yarn, mentally counting stitches in an effort to keep his mind off the time and how long it was taking his fellow passengers to get settled.

The nervousness in the pit of his stomach began to ease as the conductor, an elderly white-haired gentleman, shuffled slowly down the aisle, checking tickets.

"Will we reach Boston before noon?" That question

came from the woman with the baby seated across from him.

Len was grateful she'd asked; he was looking for answers himself.

"Hard to say with the snow and all."

"But it has to," she groaned, again voicing his own concerns. "We'll never catch our flight otherwise."

"I heard the airports are closed between Bangor and Boston," he said amiably. He scratched the side of his white head as if that would aid his concentration. "The train's running, though, and you can rest assured we'll do our best to see you make it to Boston in time."

His words reassured more than the young couple with the baby. Len's anxious heart rested a little easier, too. Glancing at the older woman in the seat next to him, he decided some conversation might help distract him.

"Are you catching a flight in Boston?"

"Oh, no," she said, tugging on the red yarn. "My daughter and her family live in Boston. I'm joining them for Christmas. Where are you headed?"

"Rawhide, Texas," Len said, letting his pride in his state show through his words.

"Texas," she repeated, not missing a stitch. "Ron and I visited Texas once. Ron wanted to see the Alamo. He's my husband...was my husband. He died this October."

"I'm sorry."

"So am I," she murmured with such utter sadness that Len had to look away. She recovered quickly and continued, "It's mind-boggling that people can fly across this country in only a few hours, isn't it?"

It was a fact that impressed Len, too, but he was more grateful than astonished. He felt even more appreciative when the whistle pierced the chatter going on about him. Almost immediately the train started to move, then quickly gained speed. Everyone aboard seemed to give a collective sigh of relief.

Len and the widow chatted amicably for several minutes and eventually exchanged names. Cathy asked him a couple of questions, about Texas and the navy, and he asked her a few. After a while, their conversation died down and they returned to their own thoughts.

The train traveled at a slow but steady pace for an hour or so. The unrelenting snow whirled around them, but the passengers were warm and cozy. For all the worry this storm had caused earlier, it didn't seem nearly as intimidating from inside the train. Relaxed, Len stretched out his legs, confident that with a little luck, he'd connect with the flight out of Logan International.

The train stopped now and then at depots on the way. Each stop resulted in a quick exchange of passengers. Len noticed that the storm appeared to have changed people's holiday plans; far more exited the train than entered. The brief stops lasted no more than ten minutes, and soon there were a number of vacant seats in the passenger car. Before long Len heard the conductor say they'd be crossing into New Hampshire.

Len figured you could fit all of these tiny New England states inside Texas. He'd seen cattle ranches that were larger than Rhode Island! The thought produced a pang of homesickness. The song sure got it right—there's no place like home for the holidays. His life belonged to the navy now, but he was a Texas boy through and through.

"Do you have someone at home waiting for you?" Cathy asked him.

"My family," Len told her, and added, prematurely, "and my fiancée." Saying the words produced a happiness in him that refused to be squelched.

"How nice for you."

"Very nice," he said. Then thinking it might help ease his mind, he opened the side zipper of his carry-on bag and pulled out Amy's most recent letter, dated two weeks earlier.

Dear Len,

I waited until ten for you to phone, then realized it was eleven your time and you probably wouldn't be calling. I was feeling low about it, then received your letter this afternoon. I'm glad you decided to write. You say you're not good at writing letters, but I disagree. This one was very sweet. It's nice to have something to hold in my hand, that I can read again and again, unlike a telephone conversation. While it's always good to hear the sound of your voice, when we hang up, there's nothing left.

Everything's going along fine here at home and at work. For all my complaining about not finding a more glamorous job, I've discovered I actually enjoy being part of the nursing-home staff. The travel agency that didn't hire me is the one to lose out.

Did I tell you we had quite a stir last week? Mr. Perkins exposed himself in the middle of a pinochle game. All the ladies were outraged, but I noticed that the sign-up sheet for pinochle this Thursday is full. Mrs. MacPherson lost her teeth, but they were eventually found. (You don't want to know where.) I still have my lunch in Mr. Danbar's room; he seems to enjoy my company, although he hasn't spoken a word in three years. I chatter away and tell him all about you and me and how excited I am that you're coming home for Christmas.

I was pleased that your mother asked me if I wanted to tag along when she and your dad pick you up at the airport on Christmas Eve. I'll be there, you know I will—which brings me to something else. Something I've been wanting to ask you for a long time.

Do you remember my joke about sailors having a woman in every port? You laughed and reminded me that, as a submariner, you didn't see that many ports above water. Bangor's a long way from Rawhide, though, isn't it? I guess I'm asking you about other women.

Well, I'd better close for now. I'll see you in two weeks and we can talk more then.

Love,
Amy

Len folded the letter and slipped it back inside the envelope. Amy shouldn't need to ask him about other women. He didn't know what had made her so insecure, but he'd noticed the doubt in her voice ever since he returned in September.

The diamond ring should relieve her worries. He smiled just thinking about it. He could hardly wait to see the look on her face.

Cathy set her knitting aside and stared sightlessly out the train window. The snow obliterated everything, not that the scenery interested her. Try as she might, she couldn't stop thinking about Ron.

Other years, she'd been working in her kitchen Christmas Eve day, baking cookies and pies, getting ready for the children and grandchildren to arrive. As a surprise—although it had long since ceased to be one—she'd always baked Ron a lemon meringue pie, his favorite. And he'd always pretend he was stunned that she'd go to all that trouble just for him.

Christmas had been the holiday her husband loved most. He was like a kid, decorating the outside of the house with strand upon strand of colorful lights. Last year he'd outdone all his previous efforts, as if he'd known even then that he wouldn't be here this Christmas.

She remembered how, every year, Ron had wanted to put up the tree right after Thanksgiving. She was lucky if she could hold him off until it was officially December.

It took them an entire day to decorate the tree. Not that

they ever chose such a large one. Trimming their Christmas tree was a ritual that involved telling each other stories about past Christmases, recalling where each decoration came from—whether it was made by one of the girls or bought on vacation somewhere or given to them by a friend. It wasn't just ornaments, baubles of glass and wood and yarn, that hung from the evergreen branches but memories. They still had several from when they were first married, back in 1957. And about ten years ago, Cathy had cross-stitched small frame ornaments with pictures of everyone in the family. It'd taken her months and Ron was as proud of those tiny frames as if he'd done the work himself.

Memories… Cathy couldn't face them this Christmas. All she could do was hope they brought her comfort in the uncertain future.

Since he'd retired from the local telephone company four years ago, Ron had used his spare time puttering around his wood shop, building toys for the grandchildren. Troy and Peter had been thrilled with the race cars he'd fashioned from blocks of wood. Ron had taken such pride in those small cars. Angela and Lindsay had adored the dollhouse he'd carefully designed and built for them. The end table he'd started for Cathy remained in his wood shop unfinished. He'd longed to complete it, but the chemotherapy had drained away his strength, and in the months that followed, it was enough for him just to make it through the day.

Ron wouldn't be pleased with her, Cathy mused. She'd made only a token effort to decorate this year. No tree, no lights on the house. She'd set out a few things—a crèche on the fireplace mantel and the two cotton snowmen Madeline had made as a craft project years ago when she was in Girl Scouts.

Actually Cathy couldn't see the point of doing more. Not when it hurt so much. And not when she'd be leaving, anyway. She did manage to bake Madeline's favorite short-bread cookies, but that had been the only real baking she'd done.

Resting her head against the seat, Cathy closed her eyes. She tried to let the sound of the train lull her to sleep, but memories refused to leave her alone, flashing through her mind in quick succession. The sights and sounds of the holidays in happier times. Large family dinners, the house filled with the scents of mincemeat pies and sage dressing. Music, too; there was always plenty of music.

Madeline played the piano and Gloria, their oldest, had been gifted with a wonderful voice. Father and daughter had sung Christmas carols together, their voices blending beautifully. At least one of their three daughters had made it home for the holidays every year. But Gloria couldn't afford the airfare so soon after the funeral, and Jeannie was living in New York now and it was hard for her to take time off from her job, especially when she'd already asked for two weeks in order to be with her father at the end. Madeline would have come, Cathy guessed, if she'd asked, but she'd never do that.

*Dear God,* she prayed, *just get me through the next three days.*

Matthew McHugh's patience was shot. The cranky baby from the station was in the same car and hadn't stopped fussing yet. Matthew's head throbbed with the beginnings of a killer headache. His argument with Pam played over and over in his mind until it was so distorted he didn't know what to think anymore.

If Pam was upset about his being gone this close to Christmas, he could only imagine what she'd say when he arrived home hours later than scheduled.

He could picture it now. His parents, Pam and the kids, all waiting for him to pull into the driveway so they could eat dinner. When he did walk in the house, they'd glare at

him as though he'd stayed away just to inconvenience
them. He'd seen it happen before. As though he were somehow personally responsible for weather conditions and canceled flights.

As for Pam's complaining about having to do all the
shopping and cooking herself, he didn't understand it. If
she preferred, they could order one of those take-out Christmas dinners from the local diner. She didn't need to do all
this work if she didn't want to. The choice was hers. He
couldn't care less if the jellied salad was homemade or
came out of a container. Pam was putting pressure on herself.

The same thing applied to inviting his parents for Christmas Eve dinner. He wasn't the one who'd asked them. That
had been Pam's doing. His mom and dad lived less than
an hour away; they could stop by the house any time they
wanted. To make a big deal out of having a meal together
on Christmas Eve was ridiculous to him, especially if Pam
was going to bitch about it.

The baby cried again. Matt clenched his fists and tried
to hold on to his patience. The infant wasn't the only irri-
tation, either. A little girl, five or so, was standing on the
seat in front of his, staring at him.

"What's your name?" she asked.

"Scrooge."

"My name's Kate."

"Shouldn't you be sitting down, Kate?" he asked pointedly, hoping the kid's mother heard him and took action.
She didn't.

"It's going to be Christmas tomorrow," she said, ignor-
ing his question.

"So I hear." He attempted to look busy, too busy to be
bothered.

The kid didn't take the hint.

"Santa Claus is coming to Grandma's house."

"Wonderful." His voice was thick with sarcasm. "Don't you know it's impolite to stare?"

"No." The kid flashed him an easy smile. "I can read."

"Good for you."

"Do you want me to read you *How the Grinch Stole Christmas*? It's my favorite book."

"No."

An elderly black couple sat across the aisle from him. The woman scowled disapprovingly, her censure at his attitude toward the kid obvious. "Why don't you read to her?" Matt suggested, motioning to the woman. "I've got work to do."

"You're working?" shrieked Kate-the-pest.

"Yes," came his curt reply, "or trying to." He couldn't get any blunter than that.

"Can I read you my story?" Kate asked the biddy across the aisle from him. Matt flashed the old woman a grin. Served her right. Let *her* deal with the kid. All Matt wanted was a few moments' peace and quiet while he mulled over what was going to happen once he got home.

Some kind of commotion went on in front of him. The little girl whimpered, and he felt a sense of righteousness. Kate's mother had apparently put her foot down when the kid tried to climb out of her seat. Good, now maybe she'd leave him and everyone else alone. If he'd been smart he would have pretended he was asleep like the man sitting next to him.

"Mom said I have to stay in my seat," Kate said, tears glistening as she peered over the cushion at him. All he could see was her watery blue eyes and the top of her head with a fancy red bow.

Matt ignored her.

"Santa's going to bring me a—"

"Listen, kid, I don't care what Santa's bringing you. I've got work to do and I don't have time to chat with you. Now kindly turn around and stop bothering me."

Kate frowned at him, then plunked herself back in her seat and started crying.

Several people condemned him with their eyes, not that it concerned Matt. If they wanted to entertain the kid, fine, but he wanted no part of it. He had more important things on his mind than what Santa was bringing a spoiled little brat with no manners.

The train had been stopped for about five minutes. "Where are we now?" Kelly asked, gently rocking Brittany in her arms. The baby had fussed the entire time they'd been on the train. Nothing Kelly did calmed her. She wasn't hungry; her diaper was clean. Kelly wondered if she might be teething. A mother was supposed to know these things, but Kelly could only speculate.

It helped that the train was becoming less crowded. With the storm, people seemed to be short-tempered and impatient. The guy who looked like a salesman was the worst; in fact, he was downright rude. She felt sorry for Kate and her mother. Kelly appreciated what it must be like traveling alone with a youngster. She'd never be able to do this without Nick. Frankly, she didn't know how anyone could travel with a baby and no one to help. An infant required so much *stuff*. It took hours just to organize and pack it all.

"According to the sign, we're in Abbott, New Hampshire," Nick informed her.

Kelly glanced out the window, through the still-falling snow. "Oh, Nick, look! This is one of those old-fashioned stations." The redbrick depot had a raised platform with several benches tucked protectively against the side, shielded from the snow by the roof's overhang. A ticket window faced the tracks and another window with many small panes looked into the waiting room.

"Hmm," Nick said, not showing any real interest.

"It's so quaint."

He didn't comment.

"I didn't know they had any of these depots left anymore. Do you think we could get off and look around a bit?"

She captured his attention with that. "You're joking, right?"

"We wouldn't have to take everything with us."

"The baby shouldn't be out in the cold."

Her enthusiasm faded. "Of course...she shouldn't."

The conductor walked down the center aisle and nodded pleasantly in Kelly's direction.

"That's a lovely old depot," she said.

"One of the last original stations in Rutherford County," he said with a glint of pride. "Built around 1880. Real pretty inside, too, with a potbellied stove and hardwood benches. They don't make 'em like this anymore."

"They sure don't," Kelly said, smiling.

"Shouldn't we be pulling out soon?" the man in the navy uniform asked, glancing at his watch.

"Anytime now," the conductor promised. "Nothing to worry about on this fine day. Snow or no snow, we're going to get you folks to Boston."

# Three

*"Have Yourself a Merry Little Christmas"*

"It's been twenty minutes," Len said, straining to see what had caused the delay. Cupping his face with his hands, he pressed against the window and squinted at the station. The snow had grown heavier and nearly obliterated the building from view. The train had been sitting outside the depot in Abbott twice as long as it had at any previous stop. Apparently the powers-that-be didn't fully grasp the time constraints he and several other passengers were under to reach Logan International. Too much was at stake if he missed his flight.

"I'm sure everything will be all right," Cathy assured

him, but he noticed that she was knitting at a frantic pace. She jerked hard on the yarn a couple of times, then had to stop and rework stitches, apparently because of a mistake.

Len saw that he wasn't the only one who seemed concerned. The cranky businessman got out of his seat and walked to the end of the compartment. He leaned over to peer out the window at the rear of the train car, as if that would tell him something he didn't already know.

"Someone's coming," he announced in a voice that said he wasn't going to be easily pacified. He wanted answers, and so did Len. Under normal circumstances Len was a patient man, but this was Christmas Eve and he had an engagement ring in his pocket.

The wind howled and snow blew into the compartment as the elderly conductor opened the door. He stepped quickly inside, then made his way to the front. "Folks, if I could have your attention a moment…"

Even before the man spoke, Len's gut told him it wasn't good news.

"We've got a problem on the line ahead."

"What kind of problem?" the sales rep demanded.

"Track's out."

A chorus of mumbles and raised voices followed.

The conductor raised his hands and the passengers fell silent. "We're doing the best we can."

"How long will it take to get it fixed?" The shout came from a long-haired guy at the front of the car. With his leather headband and fringed jacket, he resembled an overgrown hippie. He sat with a woman whose appearance complemented his—straight center-parted hair that reached the middle of her back and a long flower-sprigged dress under her heavy coat.

The conductor's face revealed doubt. "Couple of hours, possibly longer. Can't really say for sure."

"*Hours!*" Len exploded.

"We have a plane to catch," the young father cried, his anger spilling into outrage.

"The airlines arranged for us to be on the train for *this?*" the businessman shouted, not bothering to disguise his disgust. "We were better off waiting out the storm in Bangor."

"I'm sorry, but—"

"Does this podunk town have a car-rental agency?" someone asked. Len couldn't see who.

"Not right here. There's one in town, but with the storm, I'd strongly recommend none of you…"

Len didn't stick around to hear the rest. As best he could figure, he was less than sixty miles from Boston. If he could rent a car, there was a chance he might still make it to the airport on time. Moving faster than he would've thought possible, Len reached for his bag and raced off the train.

The moment he jumped onto the depot platform, a sudden blast of cold jolted him. He hunched his shoulders and kept his face down as he struggled against the icy wind to open the door. Not surprisingly, the inside of the depot was as quaint as the outside, with long rows of hardwood benches and a potbellied stove.

The stationmaster looked up as people started to flood inside. Apparently he handled the sale of tickets and whatever was available to buy—a few snack items, magazines, postcards and such. Three phones were positioned against the far wall. One bore an Out of Order sign.

A long, straggling line had already formed in front of the two working phones. Len counted ten people ahead of him and figured he had a fair chance of getting a vehicle until he remembered a friend telling him you needed to be twenty-five to rent one. His hopes sagged yet again. He was a year too young. Discouraged, he dropped out of line.

His nerves twisting, he sat on a hard wooden bench away from the others. It was hopeless. Useless to try. Even if the train had arrived anywhere close to its scheduled time, there was no guarantee he'd actually have a seat on the plane. Because of the storm, the airline had tried to get him on another flight leaving four hours later. But he was flying standby, which meant the only way he would get on board was if someone didn't show.

The reservation clerk had been understanding and claimed it wasn't as unlikely as it sounded. According to her, there were generally one or two seats available and he was at the top of the list. It had all sounded promising—and now this.

Cathy Norris sat down on the bench next to him. "I guess I should call my daughter," she said.

Len didn't know if she was speaking to him or not. "I suppose I should phone home, too."

The line for the phones had dwindled to five people. Len rejoined the group and impatiently waited his turn. It seemed to take forever before he was finally able to use the phone. He thought about contacting his parents, but he'd already spoken to them once that day.

Placing the charges on a calling card, he dialed Amy's number and prayed she was at home.

"Hello."

His relief at the sound of her soft drawl was enough to make him want to weep. "Hello, Amy Sue."

"Len?" Her voice rose with happy excitement. "Where are you?" Not giving him time to answer, she continued, "Your mother phoned earlier and said your flight had been canceled. Are you in Boston?"

"Abbott, New Hampshire."

"New Hampshire? Len, for mercy's sake, what are you doing there?"

"I wish I knew. The airline put us on a train."

"Your mother told me about the storm and how they closed the airport and everything," she said. He was distracted by the people lining up behind him, but her voice sounded...sad, almost as if she knew in advance what he was about to tell her.

"There's something wrong with the tracks. It's going to take a couple of hours to repair, so there's no telling what time I'll get to Boston."

"Oh, Len." Her voice was more breath than sound. "You're not going to make it home for Christmas, are you?"

He opened his mouth to insist otherwise, but the truth was, he no longer knew. "I want to, but..."

He could feel Amy's disappointment vibrate through the telephone wire. It was agony to be so far away and not able to hold her. "I'll do whatever I can to get to the airport on time, but there's no guarantee. You know I'd do anything to be with you right now, don't you?"

She didn't answer.

"Amy?" Talking with a lineup of people waiting to use the phone was a little inhibiting.

"I'll get in touch with your parents and let them know," she whispered, and her voice broke.

"I'll call you as soon as I hear anything," he said. Then, despite a dozen people eavesdropping on his conversation, he added, "I love you, Amy."

Unfortunately the line was already dead.

He should phone home, Matt decided, and even waited his turn in the long line that formed outside the telephone booth. He was three people away when he suddenly changed his mind. He had no idea why; then again, maybe he did.

It went without saying that Pam would be furious. He could hear her lambaste him now, and frankly, he wasn't in the mood for it.

He crossed to one of the vacant benches and sat down. These old seats might look picturesque, but they were a far

ght from being comfortable. He shifted his position a
umber of times, crossed and uncrossed his legs.

As bad luck would have it, the couple with the baby sat
irectly opposite him. Matt didn't understand it. He seemed
o attract the very people who irritated him most. Thank-
ully the infant was peacefully asleep in her mother's arms.

Matt studied the baby, remembering his own children at
nat age and how happy he and Pam had been in the early
ears of their marriage. That time seemed distant now. His
issatisfaction with his job didn't help. He felt as if he was
truggling against everything that should make life good—
is family, his marriage, his work. As if he stood waist-
eep in the middle of a fast-flowing stream, fighting the
urrent.

His wife had no comprehension of the stress he experi-
nced day in and day out. According to her, he went out
f his way to make her life miserable. Lately all she did
vas complain. If he went on the road, she complained; if
e was home, she found fault with that, too.

The thought had come to him more than once these past
ew days that maybe they'd be better off living apart. He
adn't voiced it, but it was there in the back of his mind.
Jnhappy as she was, Pam must be entertaining these same
noughts. He couldn't remember the last time they'd hon-
stly enjoyed each other's company.

Restless now, he stood and walked about. The depot had
lled up, and there wasn't room enough for everyone to
it. The stationmaster was on the phone, and Matt watched
ne old man's facial expressions, hoping to get a hint of
vhat was happening.

The man removed his black hat, frowned, then nodded.
Matt couldn't read anything into that. He waited until the
ld guy had replaced the receiver. No announcement. Ap-
arently there wasn't anything new to report. Matt checked
is watch and groaned.

Thinking he might be more comfortable back on the

train, he hurried outside, rushing through the bone-chilling wind and snow to the security of the train itself. The conductor and other staff had disappeared, Matt didn't know where. Probably all snug in the comfort of some friend' home. Not so for the passengers. The wind and snow nearly blinded him. He wasn't on board more than twenty minutes when the young father hurried inside and reached for a diaper bag tucked under the seat.

"Your first kid?" Matt asked, bored and miserable. A few minutes of conversation might help pass the time. The answer was fairly obvious. He was no expert when it came to infants, but it was clear to him that this couple was far too high-strung about parenthood. To his way of thinking, once these two relaxed, their baby would, too.

The man nodded, then sat down abruptly. "I had no idea it would be like this."

"Nothing's the same after you have kids," Matt said. The train, now that it'd shut down, wasn't heated, and the piercing cold had quickly permeated the interior.

"Do you have kids?"

"Two," Matt said, and despite his mood, he grinned. "Matt McHugh." He held out his hand.

"Nick Berry."

"This isn't exactly how I expected to spend Christmas Eve."

"Me, neither," Nick said. He lifted his shoulders and rubbed his bare hands. "If it was up to me, we'd never have left Bangor, but Kelly's parents haven't seen the baby yet."

Matt grunted in understanding.

"I'd better get back inside," Nick said. "Kelly's waiting."

"I might as well go in with you." It was obvious that he wouldn't be able to stay on the train much longer. He'd come for peace and quiet and found it not worth the price of having to sit alone in the cold. The temperature wasn't the only source of discomfort; he didn't like the turn his thoughts had taken. He didn't want a divorce, but he could see that was the direction he and Pam were headed.

Matt and Nick sprinted back into the depot just as the stationmaster walked to the center of the room. Nick rejoined his wife and handed her the diaper bag.

"Folks," the old man said, raising his arms to attract their attention. "My name's Clayton Kemper and I'm here to give you as much information as I can about the situation."

"How much longer is this going to take?" the long-haired guy demanded.

"Yeah," someone else shouted. "When do we get out of here?"

"Now, folks, that's something I can't predict. The problem involves more than the storm. The tracks are out."

His words were followed by low dissatisfied murmurs.

"I realize you're anxious to be on your way, seeing it's Christmas Eve and all. But no one can tell us just how long it'll be before the repairs are finished. Our first estimate was two hours, but the repair crew ran into difficulties."

The murmurs rose in volume. "We need answers," Matt said loudly, his fists clenched. "Some of us are booked on flights."

Clayton Kemper held up his hands. "I'm sorry, folks, I really am, but like I said before, there's just no way of predicting this sort of thing. It could be another hour...or it could be till morning."

"Morning!" The grumbling erupted into a flurry of angry shouts.

"What about hotel rooms?" an older man asked, placing a protective arm around the woman beside him.

Matt watched Nick glance at his wife as he stepped forward. "That's a good question. Should we think about getting a hotel room?" It went without saying that a young family would be far more comfortable in one. "And what's available here?"

"There's a hotel in town and a couple of motels that should have a few rooms left. I can call and they'll send their shuttle vans for anyone who wants to be picked up. Same goes for the car rental agency. But—" Mr. Kemper rubbed the side of his jaw "—I can't tell you what would be best. When the repairs are finished, the train's pulling out. We won't have time to call all over town and round people up. If you're here, you go. If not, you'll need to wait for the next train."

Matt weighed his options and decided to wait it out. He was probably being too optimistic, but he'd rather take his chances at the depot. His choice wasn't the popular one. The majority of those on the train decided to get hotel rooms. Within ten minutes, the depot had emptied, leaving twenty or so hardy souls willing to brave the rest of the afternoon.

"What about you two?" Matt asked Nick, glancing at the younger man's wife and baby. He'd expected Nick to be among the first to seek more comfortable accommodations.

"Kelly thinks we should stay."

"It could be a long hard afternoon," Matt felt obliged to remind him. Later, when Nick and his wife changed their minds, there likely wouldn't be any rooms left. But that was none of his affair.

Matt's gaze went to the telephones. He probably should phone Pam, but the prospect brought him no pleasure. He'd wait until he had a few more pertinent details. No use upsetting her this soon. She had four hours yet before she needed to know he wasn't on his scheduled flight. In this instance ignorance was bliss.

"Mother...oh dear, this isn't working out the way I'd hoped." Madeline's distress rang over the wire.

Cathy's thoughts echoed her daughter. She pressed the telephone to her ear. "I don't want you to worry."

"I have every right to worry," Madeline snapped. "I should have come up there and gotten you myself."

"Nonsense." As far as Cathy was concerned, that would only have made matters worse. The last thing she wanted was to take her daughter away from her family on Christmas Eve.

"But Daddy would—" Madeline abruptly cut off the rest of what she was about to say.

"I'm perfectly fine."

"You're in the middle of a snowstorm on Christmas Eve. You're stuck without family, alone in some train depot in a dinky town in New Hampshire. You are not fine, Mother."

*Alone.* The word leaped out of her daughter's mouth and hit Cathy hard. Hard enough that she took an involuntary step backward. Alone. That was how she'd felt since Ron's death. It seemed as though she wandered from day to day without purpose, linked to no one, lost, confused. And consumed by a grief so painful it virtually incapacitated her. All she had was the promise that time would eventually ease this ache in her heart.

"The entire situation is horrible," Madeline continued.

"What would you have me do? Scream and shout? Yell at the stationmaster who's done nothing but be as helpful and kind as possible? Is that what you want?"

Her question was followed by Madeline's soft unhappy sigh.

"I feel so incredibly guilty," her daughter confessed after a moment.

"Why in heaven's name should you feel anything of the sort?" It was ludicrous that Madeline was blaming herself for these unfortunate circumstances.

"But, Mother, you're with strangers, instead of family, and I'd hoped—"

"Now stop," Cathy said in her sternest voice. "None of this is your fault. In any case, I'm here in Abbott and perfectly content. I brought my knitting with me and there are plenty of others for company."

"But it's Christmas Eve," Madeline protested.

Cathy closed her eyes and inhaled sharply. "Do you honestly believe any Christmas will ever be the same for me without your father?"

"Oh, Mom." Her daughter's voice fell. "Don't mention Daddy, please. It's so hard without him."

"But life goes on," Cathy said, doing her best to sound brave and optimistic.

"I'd wanted to make everything better for you."

"You have," Cathy told her gently. "I couldn't have stayed at the house alone. I'd rather be in this depot with strangers than spending Christmas with memories I'm not ready to face. And sometime tonight or tomorrow, I'll be with all of you. Now let's stop before we both embarrass ourselves."

"You'll phone as soon as the tracks are repaired?"

"The minute I hear, you'll be the first to know."

"Brian and I and the girls will come down to the depot for you."

"Fine, sweetheart. Now don't you worry, okay?"

Madeline hesitated, then whispered, "I love you, Mom."

"I love you, too. Now promise me you won't fret."

"I'll try."

"Good." After a few words of farewell, Cathy replaced the receiver and returned to her seat. The depot was warm, thanks to the small stove. Those who'd stayed had taken up residence on the hardwood benches. As Cathy reached for her knitting, she battled back a fresh wave of depression.

Madeline was right. It was a dreadful situation, being

tuck in a train depot this day of all the days in the year. She glanced around at the others. They appeared just as miserable as she.

Could this really be Christmas?

# *Four*

*"The Most Wonderful Day of the Year"*

"Hi." A little girl with pigtails and a charming toothless smile sauntered up to Cathy.

"Hello," Cathy said in a friendly voice. Not including the baby, two children remained in the depot. A girl and a boy. The girl bounced about the room like a red rubber ball, but the boy remained glued to his parents' sides.

"What are you doing?" the child asked, slipping onto the wooden bench next to her.

"Knitting. This is a sweater for my granddaughter. She's about your age."

"I'm five."

"So is Lindsay."

"I can read. The kindergarten teacher told Mommy I'm advanced for my age."

"That's wonderful. I'll bet your mother and father are very proud of you." Cathy smiled at the youngster while her fingers continued to work the colorful yarn.

The little girl's head drooped slightly. "My mommy and daddy are divorced now."

Cathy felt the child's confusion and pain. "That's too bad."

She nodded, looking wise beyond her years. "We're going to spend Christmas with my grandma Gibson in Boston."

"Kate." A frazzled young woman approached the little girl. "I hope you weren't bothering this lady."

"Not at all," Cathy assured her.

"My grandma said Santa was coming tonight and bringing me lots of presents." Kate's sweet face lit up with excitement. "Santa'll still come, won't he, even if the train is late?"

"Of course he will," the child's mother told her in a tone that suggested this wasn't the first time she'd reassured her daughter.

"He'll find us even in the storm?"

"He has Rudolph's nose to guide his sleigh, remember?"

Kate nodded.

Cathy let her knitting rest in her lap.

"Can I read to you?" the youngster asked, her eyes huge. "Please?"

"Why, I can't think of anything I'd enjoy more." Cathy could, but it was clear the restless child needed something to take her mind off the situation, and she was happy to listen. Having grandchildren, she could well appreciate the difficulty of keeping a five-year-old entertained in conditions such as these.

Kate raced for her backpack and returned a moment later with her precious book.

"Thank you," Kate's mother whispered. "I'm Elise Jones."

"Hello, Elise. Cathy Norris."

Kate scooted onto the bench between Cathy and her mother and eagerly opened the book. She placed her finger on the first word and started reading aloud with a fluency that suggested this was a much-read and much-loved story.

Cathy smiled down on the little girl. Soon all this frustration and delay would be over. Mr. Kemper would come out from behind his desk and announce that the tracks had been repaired and they'd be on their way. In a few hours she'd be with Madeline and her family, all of this behind her. Somehow, listening to Kate read soothed her, made her feel that today's problems were tolerable. Inconvenient but definitely tolerable.

Kate's voice slowly faded and her eyes closed. She slumped over, her head against Cathy's side. Seconds later the book slipped from her lap and onto the floor.

"Oh, thank heaven, she's going to take a nap, after all," Elise whispered, getting carefully to her feet. She lifted Kate's small legs onto the bench and tucked a spare sweater beneath her head.

"Children can be quite a handful," Cathy murmured, remembering the first time she and Ron had watched their two granddaughters for an entire day while Madeline and Brian attended an investment workshop. The kids had been picked up by four that afternoon, but she and Ron went to bed before eight o'clock, exhausted.

"Being a single mother is no piece of cake," Elise told her. "When Greg and I divorced, I didn't have a clue what would happen. Then he lost his job and had to manage on his unemployment check. He just started working again— but he's so far behind on everything. Now he's having trouble making the child-support payments on time, which only complicates things.'' Embarrassed she looked away as if she regretted what she'd said. ''We wouldn't have Christmas if it wasn't for my mother. I certainly can't afford gifts this year.''

The pain that flashed in the younger woman's eyes couldn't be hidden. Cathy realized that, in many ways, Elise's divorce had been as devastating as a death. Feeling a kinship with her, she reached over and squeezed her hand.

Elise recovered quickly, then said with forced enthusiasm, ''I've always wanted to know how to knit.''

''Would you like me to teach you?'' Cathy asked, seizing upon the idea. She'd successfully taught her own three daughters and carried an extra set of needles in her knitting bag. Now was ideal, seeing as they had nothing but time on their hands and Kate was sleeping.

''Now?'' Elise asked, flustered. ''I mean, I'd love to, but are you sure it isn't too much trouble?''

''Of course not. I've found knitting calms my nerves, especially these past few months since my husband died.''

''I'm sorry about your husband,'' Elise said, real sympathy in her voice.

''Yes, I am, too. I miss him dreadfully.'' With a sense of purpose Cathy reached for her spare needles. ''Would you like to start now?''

Elise nodded. ''Why not?''

Cathy pulled out a ball of yarn. ''Then let me show you how to cast on stitches. It isn't the least bit difficult.''

Len had trouble not watching the clock. They'd been in Abbott a total of four hours, with no further word regarding their situation. The stationmaster, Clayton Kemper, had turned out to be a kindhearted soul. He'd made a fresh pot of coffee and offered it to anyone who wanted a cup, free of charge.

Len had declined. Stressed as he was, the last thing he needed was caffeine. Plenty of others took advantage of

Kemper's generosity, though. They were a motley group, Len noted. The widow, dressed in her gray wool coat with her knitting and her sad but friendly smile. The divorced mother and her little girl. The grumpy sales rep. The young couple with the baby, the hippie and his wife, the elderly black couple plus an assortment of others.

Kemper walked by with the coffeepot on a tray. "You sure I can't interest you in a cup, young man?"

"I'm sure."

"I found a deck of cards. How about that?"

Len nodded eagerly. "That'd be great." Cards would be a welcome way to pass the time. He sometimes played solitaire and enjoyed two or three different versions of the game. At the mention of cards, the sales rep, who sat close by, looked up from his laptop. Maybe Len could talk two or three of the others into a game of pinochle or poker.

"You play pinochle?" he asked Matt.

"And canasta, hearts, bridge—whatever you want."

"I wouldn't mind playing," Nick volunteered.

"Come to think of it, I've got an old card table in the back room," Kemper said when he returned with the cards. "And a couple of chairs, too, if you need 'em. I should have thought of this earlier. You folks must be bored out of your minds."

A fourth man joined them, and with a little rearranging they soon had the table set up. That was followed by the sound of cards being shuffled and the occasional scrape of a chair as they settled down to a friendly game of pinochle.

Kelly Berry's arms ached from holding the baby. The carrier seat was still on the train, but she hadn't asked Nick to bring it in. He'd already gone outside once and seemed reluctant to venture into the storm again. Besides, he was busy playing cards.

Kelly wondered, not for the first time, if they'd *ever* adjust to parenthood. The whole experience was so…different rom what she'd expected. Desperately longing for a child of their own, they'd dreamed and hungered to the point that Kelly felt their marriage would be incomplete without a amily. Now, after three months with a fussy, colicky in-ant, she was ready to admit her spirits were the lowest hey'd been in years.

She'd always believed a baby would bring her and Nick closer together. The baby would be a living symbol of their ove and commitment to each other, the culmination of their marriage. Instead, Brittany seemed to have driven a wedge between them. Not long ago their world had revolved en-irely around each other; these days, it revolved around Brittany. Caring for the baby demanded all their energy, all heir time.

Her arms tightened around her daughter, and a surge of love filled her heart. She and Nick felt overwhelmed be-cause this was so new, Kelly told herself. In a few months everything would be easier—for both of them. While con-fident of Nick's love, Kelly knew he found it difficult to deal with the changes that had come into their marriage since the adoption.

"Would you like me to hold the baby for a while?" The older woman sat down next to her. "I'm Cathy Norris. You must be exhausted."

"Kelly Berry." She hesitated. "You wouldn't mind?"

"Not at all," Cathy said, taking the sleeping infant from her arms. She gazed down at Brittany and smiled. "She's certainly beautiful, and her little red outfit is delightful."

"Thank you," Kelly said, truly grateful. She'd enjoyed dressing Brittany for the holiday season. She could've spent a fortune if Nick had let her, but her ever-practical husband had been the voice of reason. Not that *he* wasn't guilty of spoiling their daughter.

"She certainly resembles your husband."

Kelly glowed with happiness. "I think so, too."

With an ease that Kelly envied, Cathy Norris held Brittany against her shoulder, gently rubbing her back. Brittany shifted her head to one side and her tiny mouth made small sucking sounds. Once more Kelly's heart stirred with love.

She felt someone's gaze and glanced up to find Nick watching her. When he realized he had her attention, he smiled. His eyes softened as he looked at their daughter.

They *would* be all right, Kelly thought. This was their dream; it was just that after waiting and planning all these years, they hadn't been quite as ready for the reality as they'd assumed.

Clayton Kemper walked out of the station and returned almost immediately, a shovel in his hand. "Good news!" he shouted.

Every head in the room shot up, every face alight with expectation, Kelly's included. Some people were already on their feet, reaching for bags of colorfully wrapped gifts.

"The storm's died down. It's stopped snowing."

"Does that mean we can get out of here any sooner?" Matt McHugh demanded.

"Well, it's bound to help the repair crew."

The happy anticipation sank to the pit of Kelly's stomach. *Oh, please,* she prayed, *don't let us end up spending our first Christmas with Brittany stuck in a train depot. Don't let this be our Christmas.*

# *Five*

*"O Christmas Tree"*

The news that the snow had stopped falling should have cheered Len Dawber, but it didn't. Instead, his mood took an immediate dive. He'd figured that with the storm passing, the train would leave soon. It didn't appear to be the case.

His interest in the card game died and he got up to give his seat to someone else, but no one seemed keen to play anymore. Before long, Nick Berry had the deck of cards and sat alone, flipping through them in a listless game of solitaire.

His frustration mounting, Len approached the counter. Clayton Kemper glanced up. "Can I get you anything?"

"How about some information?" Matt McHugh asked, moving to Len's side. "We've been here six hours. There must be *something* you can tell us by now." He clenched his fist and rested it on the counter. "You've got to realize how impossible this situation is for us."

Kemper shrugged helplessly. "I don't know what to tell you."

"Isn't there someone you could phone?" The plaintive voice of a woman came from behind them. Len looked over his shoulder and recognized the mother of the little boy, who still clung to her side.

"Find out what you can," Matt insisted. "You owe us that much."

"Surely there's someone you can call," the elderly black man said.

Tension filled the room as more people stood up and started walking about. The baby Cathy Norris held awoke suddenly and shattered the air with a piercing cry. Cathy tried to quiet the infant, but it did no good. The young mother couldn't do any better. The baby's cries clawed at already taut nerves.

"Kindly keep that baby quiet, would you?" Len wasn't sure who'd said that; painful as the baby's shrieking was, he felt a fleeting sympathy for the mother.

"Do something," Nick snapped at his wife.

"I'm trying," Kelly said, glaring back at him with a hurt look.

"I've got to get out of here," Nick said, and stalked outside, letting the door slam in his wake.

"We need information," Len pressed Kemper again.

"At least give us an idea how much longer it could be," Matt added. "In case you've forgotten, it's Christmas Eve."

Kemper was clearly at a loss and for an instant Len felt sympathy for him, too, but he felt even worse for himself. He'd been looking forward to this night for weeks. He wanted it to be the most beautiful and romantic evening of his life. Instead, he'd probably be spending it in this train station somewhere in New Hampshire.

Kemper raised his hands to quiet the murmurs of discontent. "I'll make a few phone calls and see what I can find out."

"You should have done that long before now," Matt said irritably.

Len was in full agreement. This damned waiting had gone on long enough. The minute he had a definite answer, he'd call Amy again. Even if he *didn't* have an answer, he was phoning Amy. He needed to hear the sound of her voice, needed to know this nightmare would soon be over and they'd be together—if not for Christmas, then soon.

Len returned to his seat and Matt followed him. "This isn't exactly my idea of Christmas Eve," the older man muttered, more to himself than his companion.

"I don't think any of us could have anticipated this."

It didn't take Kemper long to connect with someone, Len noticed. The stationmaster was on the phone five minutes. He nodded once in a while, then scowled and wrote something down on a piece of paper. When he'd finished, he walked toward the potbellied stove.

Every eye in the room followed him. "Well," he said, with a deep expressive sigh, "there really isn't any news I can give you."

"No news is good news?" Cathy suggested hopefully.

"No news is no news," Matt McHugh returned tartly.

"You were talking to someone," Len said. "They must've had something to say...."

"Only what I found out earlier, that the break in the line is more serious than was originally determined."

"Isn't there anything you can suggest? How long should we expect to wait? Give us your best estimate. Surely you've seen breakdowns like this before." Len's voice thinned with frustration. He noticed a number of people nodding as he spoke.

"Well," Kemper said thoughtfully, "you're right, I have seen plenty of breakdowns over the years. Each one's different. But we've got a full crew working on this one, despite the fact that it's Christmas Eve."

"That's encouraging, anyway," Elise Jones said. "It isn't like any of us planned to spend the holidays here, you know."

"I know, I know." Kemper looked out over the group and seemed to recognize that he wouldn't be off the hook until he gave these people some kind of answer. "My best guess is sometime after midnight."

"Midnight!" Matt shouted.

He wasn't the only one who reacted with anger. But Len barely reacted at all; he felt as though the wind had been knocked clear out of him. Slowly he sank onto the bench and closed his eyes. He no longer knew if the airline could even get him a seat. Because of the snowstorm he'd missed his original flight. Because of the train's delay, he hadn't made the standby flight, either. Nor could he book another. Not until he could give the airline a time.

This felt like the worst day of his life.

Nick knew he was a fool, snapping at his wife in front of a room full of strangers and then stalking out of the train depot like a two-year-old having a tantrum. He'd caught the shocked look in Kelly's eyes. It was uncharacteristic behavior for him, but he'd just been feeling so…on edge. Then he'd lost control because someone had shouted at Kelly to keep Brittany quiet.

What upset him was that he'd been thinking the same

thing himself. He wanted her to do something, anything, to stop Brittany's crying. The baby had been contentedly asleep for a few hours, and he supposed he'd been lulled into a false sense of peace. Then she'd awakened, and it seemed that every ounce of composure he'd managed to scrape together had vanished.

He'd say one thing for his daughter. She had an incredible sense of timing. Why she'd pick that precise moment to start wailing, he'd never know. She was a fragile little thing, but obviously had the lungs of a tuba player.

It had felt as though everyone in the room was glaring at him and Kelly with malice, although in retrospect, he thought his own frustrations had probably made him misread their reactions. Everything in life had come hard for Nick; why should fatherhood be any different? He'd been raised in a series of foster homes and the only reason he'd been able to go on with his schooling was because of a scholarship. He'd graduated while holding down two part-time jobs and now worked as a scientist for a pharmaceutical company. He'd met Kelly when they were both in college. He still considered it a miracle that this beautiful woman loved him. For years now, her love had been the constant in his life, his emotional anchor, his sanctuary.

The intense cold had soaked through his coat. He kicked at the snow, depressed and angry with himself. Kelly deserved a better husband, and Brittany sure as hell needed a more loving father.

He was about to go back inside the station when the door opened and Clayton Kemper walked out.

"You're leaving?" Nick asked, shocked that the station-master would desert them at a time like this.

Clayton Kemper looked more than a little guilty. "My shift was over an hour ago and the missus is wanting me home."

Talk about deserting the ship. "Someone else is coming, right?"

"Oh, sure. Don't you worry. Someone'll be by to check up on you folks, but it might not be for a while." Having said that, he headed down the steps, then glanced back over his shoulder and called, "Merry Christmas."

Nick stared at the man in disbelief. This had to be the worst Christmas of his entire life! Trapped with a cranky newborn and a wife who refused to see reason. If it'd been up to him, the three of them would at least have been in a motel room, comfortable and warm. But Kelly hadn't wanted to leave the station, certain the repairs wouldn't take long. Now it was too late. The guy with the long hair and his wife had already made inquiries. Apparently every hotel for miles around was full.

This optimistic bent of Kelly's had always been a problem. He'd been ready to give up on the fertility clinic long before she agreed. The expense had been horrific, and he didn't mean just the financial aspects. Emotionally Kelly was a wreck two weeks out of every month. Only when he was able to talk her into accepting their situation and applying to an adoption agency had she gotten off the emotional roller coaster.

Nick had almost given up hope himself—and then they received the phone call about Brittany. That five-minute conversation had changed their lives forever.

He found himself grinning at the memory. Kelly was the one who'd been cool and calm while he'd sat there trembling. He'd never experienced any excitement even close to what he'd felt when he learned they finally had a baby.

The first instant he saw Brittany, he'd been swept by a love so powerful it was beyond comprehension. Yet here he was, three months later, acting like a dolt and snapping at his wife in public.

That wasn't his only offense, either. For most of the afternoon, he'd ignored Kelly and the baby, wanting to escape them both. He wasn't proud of himself; he'd ignored their needs, leaving Kelly to care for their daughter on her own while he brooded and behaved like a spoiled child.

With that in mind, he boarded the train, walked down the narrow aisle and got the baby seat down from the storage compartment. Kelly's arms must be tired from holding Brittany. He wished he'd thought of this sooner.

Hauling in a deep breath, he walked back into the station and stomped the snow from his boots. When he looked up, he discovered Kelly staring at him, her lips tight, but her eyes forgiving.

"I'm sorry," he whispered as he sat beside her. He gazed down at Brittany, who gazed back at him, her blue eyes wide and curious. His daughter seemed to recognize him, and she, at least, didn't know enough to realize what a cantankerous fool he'd been the past few hours. He offered her his finger, which she gripped eagerly with her little hand.

"I'm sorry, too," Kelly whispered back, sounding close to tears.

Nick set the baby seat on the floor and placed his arm around his wife's shoulders. She leaned her head against him. "I don't know what came over me," he murmured. "I wish we were anyplace but here."

"Me, too," Kelly said.

"Amy?"

Len felt a surge of relief and unmistakable joy at the sound of her "hello."

"Are you in Boston?" she asked excitedly. "When can you catch a flight home?"

"I'm still in Abbott," Len said, his happiness evaporating quickly with the reality of this long day. He was trapped, a hostage to circumstances beyond his control.

"You're still in Abbott?" Amy sounded ready to weep. "Oh, Len, will you ever get home for Christmas?"

"I don't know," he told her, trying to keep his own hopes alive—and failing. It seemed everything was against him

"Yes," he said suddenly, emphatically. For a moment he didn't know where this optimism had come from. Then he did. It was his overwhelming need to be with Amy. "I *will* get home for Christmas." He wasn't about to let the storm, the damaged tracks or anything else ruin his leave. "I'll be home for Christmas, Amy. You can count on it."

He could almost feel her spirits rise. "Your girl in Rawhide will be waiting for you, sailor man."

"You're more than my girl in Rawhide," Len said. "You're my one and only girl. Period!"

She said nothing after his declaration. "Do you mean that, Len?" she finally asked.

"With all my heart." He was tempted to tell her about the diamond, but that would ruin his surprise, and he didn't want to propose over the phone. It just didn't seem near good enough. He wanted her to see the love in his eyes and watch her face when she saw the ring.

"Oh, Len," she whispered.

"Listen, would you call my mom and dad and tell them I still don't know when I'll be home?"

"Sure. Listen, since you can't be here, I'll go back to the nursing home tonight and play the piano for everyone. They wanted to sing Christmas carols but couldn't find any staff willing to take time away from their families."

Len loved her all the more for her generous heart.

"I can't see sitting around home and moping," she explained.

"Sing a Christmas carol for me."

"I will," she said, and her voice softened.

There was a beep in his ear and Len knew he had only a couple of minutes left on his calling card.

"Oh, Len," Amy said. "Time's running out."

"Remember, I'll see you as soon as I can," he said, ready to hang up.

"Len, Len…"

"Yes? What is it?"

"Len," she said, her voice catching, "I…love you. I was going to wait until tonight to tell you, but I want you to know right now. You might be in New Hampshire and me here in Rawhide, but that doesn't matter, because you have my heart with you wherever you are."

The line went dead. Len wasn't sure if she'd hung up or if the time had simply expired.

"I love you, too, Amy," he said into the silent phone, knowing she couldn't hear the words. Somehow he was certain she could feel his heart responding to hers. Soon she'd know how very much he loved his Amy Sue.

Len replaced the receiver and turned around to face the room. Everyone seemed in a dour mood.

The door burst open just then and a smiling, lighthearted Clayton Kemper walked in. He glanced around and beamed proudly at the group of weary travelers.

"I was on my way home when I ran across this," he said cheerfully. He stuck his hand out the door and dragged in the sorriest-looking Christmas tree Len had ever seen.

One side of the evergreen was bare, the top had split and two branches spiked in opposite directions, resembling bug antennae.

"The man in the Christmas-tree lot gave it to me for a buck."

"You got overcharged," Matt McHugh muttered. His words were followed by a few short laughs and a general feeling of agreement.

"That may well be," Kemper said, not letting their lack

of enthusiasm dampen his spirit. "But it seemed to me that since you folks are stuck here on Christmas Eve, you might as well make the best of it."

"That tree looks like it's in the same shape we're in," Elise Jones said dryly.

"The tree is yours to do with as you wish," Kemper told them. "Merry Christmas to you all."

No one thought to thank him, Len noticed.

The sad little tree stood in the center of the room, bare and forlorn, wounded and ugly. He'd have to go along with Elise. The Christmas tree did resemble them—and their attitude.

Five-year-old Kate Jones walked over to it and stood with her arms akimbo, staring at the limp branches. Then, apparently having come to some sort of decision, she turned to confront the disgruntled group.

"I think it's a beautiful tree," she announced. "It just needs a little help." She removed the red bow from the top of her head and pinned it to the nearest branch.

Despite himself, Len grinned. On closer examination, the kid was right. The tree wasn't nearly as ugly as he'd first thought.

# Six

*"Sing We Now of Christmas"*

Most everyone ignored the Christmas tree, Cathy Norris mused sadly. Except for Kate… Then Kelly walked over and silently added a rattle. She took her time finding just the right spot for it, choosing to hang it directly in the middle, opposite Kate's hair bow.

Turning to the others, she smiled and said, "Come on, you guys, it's Christmas Eve."

"She's right," Nick said, and joined his wife. He bounced the baby gently in his arms, and Brittany grinned and reached for his bright green muffler. Nick removed it, handed the baby to Kelly and placed the muffler on the tree, stretching it out as if it were the finest decorative strand. He wove it between the lower branches of the fir, the wool fringe dangling like green wool tinsel.

Len surveyed the tree, then stepped up and added his white cap, settling it near the top, where it sat jauntily.

The elderly black man moved forward next and added his tie clasp. He clipped it to the branch in an upright position like a clothespin, stepped back and nodded once, apparently pleased with the effect. "Hey, this tree doesn't look so bad."

Soon others became creative about decorating the Christmas tree. Cathy cut strips of red yarn and with Kate's help draped the strands over as many branches as they could reach.

Even the grumpy salesman pitched in. Cathy saw him with the small pair of scissors on his Swiss Army knife, folding and cutting memos into paper snowflakes, then hanging them on the tree with dental floss. Actually they looked quite attractive against the backdrop of red yarn.

It wasn't long before every branch sprouted some sort of odd decoration. True, it wasn't a traditional Christmas tree, but it seemed to possess amazing powers. The scowls and complaints of moments earlier were now replaced by smiles and animated chatter.

"I think my daughter's right," Elise said, walking over to more closely examine their handiwork. "This is actually a beautiful tree."

The little boy, around three or four, who'd stayed close by his parents the entire day, clapped in delight.

Cathy noticed several smiles.

"I'm hungry," Kate whispered to her mother.

Worrying about their situation as she had for most of the day, Cathy hadn't given any thought to food until the youngster mentioned it. She apparently wasn't the only one.

"What about dinner?" Cathy asked, glancing about the room. It looked as though they'd been left to fend for themselves. Mr. Kemper had said someone would come by to check on them, but so far no one had.

"Nothing's going to be open tonight," Matt McHugh grumbled. "Not on Christmas Eve."

"Especially not with the storm and all earlier," Len put in.

Cathy could feel the mood of the room, so recently elevated, plunge. Already those who'd moved closer to the Christmas tree were sliding away to slump on benches by the walls.

"Now, that does bring up an interesting prospect," Cathy said, speaking to the entire group for the first time. "I'm Cathy Norris, by the way. I'm going to visit my daughter and her family in Boston, and I just happened to bring along four dozen of her favorite shortbread cookies. Somehow, I don't think she'd mind my sharing them with all of you."

She brought out the tin and pried open the lid.

"My wife and I have several oranges," the elderly black man said. "We can share those. Since we're going to be eating together, it's only appropriate that we introduce ourselves. My name's Sam Givens and my wife's Louise."

"Thank you, Sam and Louise," Cathy said. "Anyone else?"

"I'm Matt McHugh. I was given a fruitcake on my last sales call," Matt surprised her by saying. "I would've thrown the damn thing out, but one of my kids likes the stuff. I can cut that up if anyone's interested."

"Well, I'm quite fond of fruitcake," Kelly Berry said.

Although the depot office was locked, the counter was free and Cathy placed the tin of cookies there. Matt took out the fruitcake and sliced it with his Swiss Army knife. Sam Givens brought over the oranges, then peeled and sectioned them.

Elise Jones collected paper towels from the rest room to use as napkins. Soon more and more food appeared. It seemed almost everyone had something to share. A plate of beautifully decorated chocolates. A white cardboard box filled with pink divinity and homemade fudge. Then a tin of peanuts and a bag of pretzels. Len added a package of cinnamon-flavored gum.

A crooked line formed and they all helped themselves, taking bits and pieces of each dish. It wasn't much, but it helped do more than dull the edge of their hunger. It proved, to Cathy at least, that there was hope for them. That banding together they could get through this and even have a good time.

"My mother's serving prime rib right about now," Elise lamented as she took an orange segment and a handful of peanuts.

"And to think she's missing out on Matt McHugh's fruitcake," Cathy said, and was delighted by the responding laugh that echoed down the line. Even Matt chuckled. An hour ago Cathy would have thought that impossible.

"I never thought I'd say this about fruitcake," the young sailor said, saluting Matt with a slice, "but this ain't half-bad."

"What about my peanuts?" the guy with long hair asked. "I spent hours slaving over a hot stove to make those."

Everyone smiled and the silly jokes continued.

"Quiet," Nick said suddenly, jumping to his feet. "I hear something."

"A train?" Matt teased.

"'Do you hear what I hear?'" Someone sang.

"I'm serious."

It didn't take Cathy long to pick up the faint sound of voices singing. "Someone's coming," she announced.

"Carolers?" Kelly asked. "On a night like this? For us?"

"No night more perfect," Cathy murmured. Years ago she and Ron had been members of the church choir. Each holiday season the choir had toured nursing homes and hospitals, giving short performances. They'd been active in their church for a number of years. Unfortunately their attendance had slipped after Ron retired, then stopped completely when he became seriously ill. And afterward…well, afterward Cathy simply didn't have the heart for it.

For the first time since the funeral, she felt the need to return. This insight was like an unexpected gift, and it had come to her at the sound of the carolers' voices.

The door opened and a group of fifteen or so entered the train depot.

"Hello, everyone." A man with a bushy gray mustache and untamed gray hair stepped forward. "I'm Dean Owen. Clayton Kemper's a friend of mine and he mentioned you folks were stranded. This is the teen choir from the Regular Baptist Church. Since we weren't able to get out last night because of the snow, we thought we'd make a few rounds this evening. How's everyone doing?"

"Great."

"As good as can be expected."

"Hangin' in there."

"I love your Christmas tree," one of the girls said. She was about sixteen, with long blond hair in a ponytail and twinkling eyes.

"We decorated it ourselves," Kate said, pointing to her hair bow. "That's mine."

"Would anyone mind if I took a picture?" the girl asked, pulling a disposable camera from her coat pocket.

"This is something that's got to be seen to be believed," Matt whispered to Cathy. "Actually I wouldn't mind having a copy of it myself."

"Me, too."

"Shall we make it a family photo?" Elise asked.

A chorus of yes's and no's followed, but within a minute the ragtag group had gathered around the tree. Cathy ran a comb through her hair and added a dash of lipstick. Others, too, reviewed their appearance as they assembled for the photograph, jostling each other good-naturedly.

What amazed Cathy were the antics that went on before the picture was taken. They behaved like a group of teenagers themselves. Len held up the V for peace sign behind Nick's head. Even Matt managed a crooked smile. For that matter, so did Cathy. Someone joked and she laughed. That made her realize how long it'd been since she'd allowed herself to be happy. *Too long. Ron wouldn't want that.*

The girl took four snapshots. Before long the development of the film had been paid for and she had a list of names and addresses to send copies of the photo. Cathy's name was there along with everyone else's. She wanted something tangible to remember this eventful day—the oddest Christmas Eve she'd spent in her entire life.

"We thought we'd deliver a bit of cheer," Dean said, once the photo arrangements were finished.

Their coming had done exactly that. The travelers gathered around without anyone's direction, positioning the benches in a way that allowed them all to see the singers.

The choir assembled in three rows of five each and began with "Silent Night," sung in three-part harmony. Cathy had heard the old carol all her life, but never had it sounded more beautiful than it did this evening. Without accompaniment, without embellishment, simple, plain—and incredibly lovely. With the beautiful words came a sense of camaraderie and joy, a sense that this night was truly special.

This *was* a holy night.

"Silent Night" was followed by "The Little Drummer Boy," then "Joy to the World," one carol flowing smoothly into another, ending with "We Wish You a Merry Christmas."

While Cathy and the others applauded loudly, Kate in a burst of childish enthusiasm spontaneously rushed forward and hugged Dean's knees. "That was so pretty," she squealed, her delight contagious.

Len jumped to his feet, continuing the applause. Soon the others stood, too, including Cathy.

The small choir seemed overwhelmed by their appreciation.

"This is the first time we ever got a standing ovation," the girl with the camera said, smiling at her friends. "I didn't realize we were that good."

"Sing more," Kate pleaded. "Do you know 'Rudolph the Red-Nosed Reindeer'?"

"Can you sing it with us?" Dean bent down and asked Kate.

The child nodded enthusiastically, and Dean had her stand in front of the choir. "Sing away."

"Join in, everyone," he suggested next, turning to face his small audience.

Cathy and the others didn't need any encouragement. Their voices blended with those of the choir as if they'd sung together for weeks. "Rudolph" led to other Christmas songs—"Silver Bells," "Deck the Halls," and the time passed quickly.

When they finished, the choir members brought out paper cups and thermoses of hot chocolate. No sooner had the hot drink been poured than the station door opened again.

"So Clayton was right." A petite older woman, with a cap of white hair and eyelids painted the brightest shade of blue Cathy had ever seen, entered the room. Two other women filed in after her.

"I'm Greta Barnes," the leader said, "and we're from the Veterans of Foreign Wars Women's Auxiliary."

"We've brought you folks dinner," another woman told them.

"Now you're talking!" Len Dawber shouted. "Sorry, folks, but a slice of fruitcake and a few pretzels didn't quite fill me up."

"Made for a great appetizer, though," Nick said.

"The food's out in the car. Would someone help carry it in?'' Greta asked. She didn't have to ask for volunteers a second time. Nick, Matt and Len were up before any of the other men had a chance. A couple of minutes later they were back inside, their arms loaded with boxes.

"It's not much,'' one of the other women said apologetically as she set a huge pot of soup on the counter. "We didn't get much notice.''

"We're grateful for whatever you brought us,'' Sam assured the women. Louise nodded in agreement.

"Luckily the family had plenty of clam chowder left over,'' the older of Greta's friends said. "The soup's a Christmas Eve tradition in our house, and I can't help it, I always cook up more than enough.''

"Eleanor's soup is the best in the state,'' Greta declared.

"There's sandwiches, too,'' the third woman said, unpacking one of the smaller boxes.

"And seeing that no one knows when the repairs on those tracks are going to be finished,'' the spry older woman added, "we decided to bring along some blankets and pillows.''

"All the comforts of home,'' Matt muttered, but the caustic edge that had laced his comments earlier in the day had vanished.

"I must say you folks are certainly good sports about all this.''

Considering that this change in attitude had only recently come about, none of them leaped to their feet to accept credit.

"Like I said earlier,'' Matt told her, speaking for the group, "we're making the best of it.''

"We're very grateful for the pillows and blankets,'' Cathy put in.

"The food, too,'' several others said.

The church choir stayed and helped pass around the sandwiches, which were delicious. Cathy ate half a tuna-salad sandwich, then half a turkey one. She was amazed at how big her appetite was. Food, like almost everything since Ron's death, had become a necessity and not an enjoyment.

When the teen choir left, it was with a cheery wave and the promise that everyone who'd asked for a picture would be sure to receive one. With a responsible kindhearted man like Dean Owen as their leader, Cathy was confident it would come about.

The soup and sandwiches disappeared quickly. Three other men helped pack up the leftovers and carted the boxes out to the car.

"You sure we can't get you anything else?" Greta asked before she headed outside.

"You've done more than enough."

"Thank Mr. Kemper for us," Len said, ready to escort the older women to their vehicle.

With many shouts of "Merry Christmas," everyone waved the Auxiliary ladies goodbye.

Len returned, leaning against the door when it closed. Cathy watched as he paused and glanced about the room. "You know," he said, not speaking to anyone in particular, "I almost feel sorry for all those people who decided to stay in hotels. They've missed out on the best Christmas Eve I can ever remember."

# Seven

*"Santa Claus Is Coming to Town"*

The station seemed unnaturally quiet after the choir and the members of the VFW Women's Auxiliary had left. The lively chatter and shared laughter that had filled the room died down to a low hum.

Matt knew he should phone home, that he'd delayed it as long as he dared. With the time difference between the east and west coasts, it wasn't quite four in the afternoon in Los Angeles. The dread that settled over him depleted the sense of well-being he'd experienced over the past few hours.

He didn't look forward to a telephone confrontation with Pam, but as far as he could see there was no avoiding one. He could almost hear her voice, starting low and quickly gaining volume until it reached a shrill, near-hysterical pitch.

He wished things could be different, but he knew she'd start in on him, and then, despite his best efforts, he'd retaliate. Soon their exchange would escalate into a full-blown fight.

His feet felt weighted as he crossed the station to the row of pay phones. He slipped his credit card through the appropriate slot, punched in his home number and waited for the line to connect.

The phone rang twice, three times, then four before the answering machine came on. Bored, he tapped his foot while he listened to the message he'd recorded earlier in the year. When he heard the signal, he was ready. "Pam, it's Matt. I'm sorry about this, but I got caught in the snowstorm that struck Maine yesterday. The flights out of Bangor were canceled, so the airline put me on a train for Boston. Now the train tracks are out and I don't have a clue when I'll be home. As soon as I reach Boston, probably sometime Christmas morning, I'll phone and let you know when to expect me. I'm sorry about this, but it's out of my control. Kiss the kids for me and I'll see you as soon as I can."

The relief that came over him at not getting caught in a verbal battle with his wife was like an unexpected gift. This wasn't how it should be, but he felt powerless to change the dynamics of their marriage. Somewhere along the road the partnership they'd once shared had fallen apart. He wasn't the only one who felt miserable; he knew that. The look in Pam's eyes as he'd walked through the house, suitcase in hand, had told him he wasn't the only one thinking about a separation.

His mood was oppressive by the time he returned to his seat.

"What about Santa?" Matt heard Kate ask her mother.

"Honey, he's still coming to Grandma's house." Kate's mother was busy making up a bed for her daughter. She placed a pillow at one end of the bench and arranged the blanket so the little girl could sleep between its folds.

"But, Mom, I'm *not* at Grandma Gibson's house—I'm *here*. Santa might not know."

Elise apparently needed a minute to think about that. "Grandma will have to tell him."

"But what if Santa decides to try to find me here, instead of leaving my presents with Grandma?"

"Kate, please, can't you just trust that you're going to get your gifts?"

Arms crossed, the child shook her head stubbornly. "No, I can't," she said, her voice as serious as the expression on her face. "You told me Daddy was going to come see me before we left and he didn't."

"Honey, I don't have any control over what your father says and does. I'm sorry he disappointed you."

Her look said it wasn't the first time mother and child had been let down.

Kate started to whimper.

"Sweetheart, please," Elise whispered. She seemed close to breaking down herself. She picked up her daughter and held her close. As she gently rocked the little girl, her eyes shone with unshed tears. "Santa won't forget you."

"Daddy did."

"No, honey, I'm sure he didn't, not really."

"Then why didn't he come like he said?"

"Because…" Elise began, then hesitated and forcefully expelled her breath. "It's complicated."

"Everything's complicated since you and Daddy divorced."

Matt felt like an eavesdropper, yet he couldn't tune out the conversation between mother and child. Part of him yearned to let Kate use his credit card to phone her father, but if he suggested that, Elise would know he'd been listening in.

Hearing Kate cry about being forgotten by her dad left Matt to wonder if this would be his own children's future should he and Pam decide to split up. He didn't want a divorce, never had. But it was obvious they couldn't continue the way they'd been going—belittling each other, arguing, eroding the foundation of their love and commitment.

"Why didn't Daddy come see me like he said he would?" Kate persisted.

Elise took her time answering. "Your daddy was embarrassed."

"Embarrassed?"

"He felt bad."

"About what?"

"Being late helping to pay the bills. He didn't come see you because…well, because I don't think he could afford to buy you anything for Christmas, and he didn't want you to be disappointed in him because he didn't have a gift."

Kate mulled that over for a while, nibbling her bottom lip. "I love him and I didn't have a gift for him, either."

"Your daddy loves you, Kate, that much I know."

"Can I talk to him myself?"

Elise took a deep breath. "You can phone him when we reach Grandma's house, and you can tell him about spending the night in the train depot. He'll want to hear about all your adventures on Christmas Eve.''

Matt considered what would happen to his relationship with his children if he and Pam went their separate ways. The love he felt for Rachel and Jimmy ran deep, and the idea of Pam having to make excuses for him...

His thoughts tumbled to an abrupt halt. That was exactly what Pam had been forced to do the afternoon he'd left for Maine. Jimmy had been counting on him to attend the school Christmas program and, instead, he'd raced off to the airport. Matt's stomach knotted, and he sat back, wiping a hand down his face.

A whispered discussion broke out between the widow and the elderly couple who'd supplied the oranges. Matt had no idea what was going on and, caught up in his own musing, didn't much care.

Not long afterward, he discovered that a few of the senior crowd had decided to take this matter of Christmas for the two children into their own hands.

Cathy walked by Kate, paused suddenly and held one hand to her ear. ''Did you hear something?'' she asked the youngster.

''Not me,'' Kate answered.

''I think it's bells.''

Elise cupped her ear. ''Reindeer feet?''

''Bells,'' Cathy returned pointedly.

''Yes,'' Louise piped up. ''It's definitely the sound of bells. What could it be?''

They weren't going to get any Academy Award nominations, but they did manage to convince the children.

''I hear bells!'' the other child called. ''I do, I do.'' It was the first time the little boy had spoken all day.

Kate sat up straight on her mother's lap. ''I hear them, too.''

Matt had to admit the two old ladies really had him going; he could almost hear them himself. Then he realized he really *could* hear the jingle of bells.

A knock sounded loudly on the station door. "I'll get it." Sam eagerly stepped to the door. He opened it a couple of inches, nodded a few times and looked over his shoulder. "Do we have a little girl named Kate here and a boy...Charlie?"

"Charles," his mother corrected.

"Kate and Charles," Sam informed the mysterious visitor no one was allowed to see. "As a matter of fact, Kate and Charles *are* here," Sam said loudly. "You do...of course. I'll see to it personally. Now don't you worry, you have plenty of other deliveries to make tonight. You'd best be on your way."

Matt glanced around and noticed that Nick Berry was missing...and he seemed to remember that their baby had a rattle with bells inside.

The room went quiet as Sam closed the door, and the jingling receded. He had a pillowcase in one hand, with a couple of wrapped gifts inside. "That was Santa Claus," he announced. "He heard that Kate and Charles were stuck here on Christmas Eve. Santa wanted them to know he hadn't forgotten them."

"Did he bring my presents?" Kate sprang off her mother's lap and ran toward Sam, still standing near the door.

Charles joined her, gazing up at the man with hopeful eyes.

"Santa wanted me to tell you he left plenty of gifts at your Grandma Gibson's house, Kate, but he didn't want you to worry that he'd missed you, so he dropped this off." He thrust his arm into the pillowcase and produced a wrapped box.

Matt recognized it right away as one he'd seen poking out of Cathy Norris's carry-on bag when she'd removed the tin of cookies.

"I believe this one is for you, Charles," Sam said. The second gift went to the four-year-old. The boy raced back to his parents and dropped to his knees. He tore into the wrapping paper, scattering pieces in all directions. The minute Charles saw the rubber dinosaur, he cried out in delight and hugged it to his chest.

Kate, on the other hand, opened her present with delicate precision, carefully removing the ribbon first and placing it on the tree. Next came the wrapping paper. Matt couldn't figure out how she did it, but she managed to pull off the Christmas wrap without tearing it even once. When she saw the Barbie doll, she looked up at her mother and smiled wonderingly.

"Daddy must have given it to Santa. This is what I told him I wanted."

"I'm sure he did," Elise was gracious enough to concur.

Matt didn't know what had gone wrong in this woman's marriage, but it wasn't difficult to see the pain that divorce had brought into her life. Could bring into his own, if he allowed it to happen.

Cathy and the elderly couple exchanged smiles that their small ploy had worked. Actually Matt was touched by their generosity; they'd obviously given up Christmas presents meant for their own grandchildren.

He wasn't sure what prompted the idea, but he reached for his briefcase. "As a matter of fact, Santa left a few goodies with me, too. Is anyone interested in a sample of the latest software from MicroChip International?"

It didn't take long to discover that a number of people were.

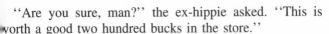
"Are you sure, man?" the ex-hippie asked. "This is worth a good two hundred bucks in the store."

"Five hundred, actually," Matt said. "Consider it compliments of the company."

"We've got extra pictures of the baby, if anyone would like," Nick offered.

"Sure," Len said. "Amy—my fiancée—is crazy about babies." He took one and so did Cathy, Elise and several others.

As had happened earlier with the food, a variety of gifts, some wrapped and others not, started to appear. The joking and laughter continued during the impromptu gift exchange. By the end, everyone had both given and received at least one gift.

Sam, who'd stayed in the background most of the day, stepped forward with a worn Bible in his hand. "This being the night of our Savior's birth," he said, "I thought we might like to listen to the account of the first Christmas."

Most people nodded in silent agreement. Sam pulled out a chair and set it close to their Christmas tree, then perched a pair of glasses on his nose.

The room hushed as he began to read. His rich resonant voice echoed through the depot. Everyone listened with an attentiveness Matt found amazing.

When he'd finished, Sam reverently closed the Bible and removed his glasses, tucking them into his shirt pocket. "It seems to me that we all have something in common with Mary and Joseph. They, too, were weary travelers and there wasn't any room for them at the inn." He paused and held up one hand. "I checked earlier and every room in this town has been booked for the night."

There were grins and murmurs at his remark. Sam got to his feet and sang the first words of "Silent Night." Everyone joined in, their voices rising in joyful sound. Matt thought he'd never heard anything so achingly beautiful, so…sincere.

As the last line died away, Sam walked over to the wall and turned out the light. The room went dim, but the outside lights cast a warm glow into the station's interior.

"It's nine o'clock," the ex-hippie announced. "I haven't been to bed this early in twenty years, but I'm more than ready to hit the hay."

His wife giggled. The two of them cuddled awkwardly on the hard bench, kissing and whispering.

Matt felt a pang of regret at seeing the closeness they shared, a closeness so sadly lacking in his own marriage. He glanced at his watch, certain that Pam would be home now, probably seething about the brief message he'd left. Nevertheless he wanted to talk to her. No, he corrected himself, he *needed* to talk to her.

Light from the window guided him to the far wall of the station, to the phones. Because it was still early, people continued to talk. He slipped his credit card through the slot and waited for the line to connect.

Pam answered on the first ring. "Hello." Her clipped tone told him she was angry, as he'd expected.

"It's Matt," he said.

"Matt?" She paused. "Matt?" she said again. "Where—"

"Merry Christmas, sweetheart," he whispered.

"How can you 'Merry Christmas' me with the kids screaming in my ear? Your parents are due any minute, and the house is a mess. The cat tipped over the Christmas tree and you're…you're…" She burst into tears.

"Pam," he said softly. "Honey, don't cry."

"I can't help it! I suppose you're in some posh hotel, ogling the cocktail waitress, while I'm here—"

"I'm not in any hotel."

"Then where are you?"

"A hundred-year-old train depot with..." Now it was is turn to pause. "With friends who were strangers not nat long ago."

"A train depot?" She sniffled and sounded unsure.

"It's a long story and I'll tell you about it when I get ome."

"You didn't phone all week."

"I know and I'm sorry, sweetheart, really sorry. It was hildish and silly of me to let our argument stand in the vay of talking to you and the kids."

"You haven't called me sweetheart in a long time."

"Too long," Matt said. "I've done a lot of thinking hese past few days, and once I'm home I want to talk to ou about making some changes."

"I've been a terrible wife," she sobbed into the phone.

"Pam, you haven't. Now stop. I love you and you love ne, and we're going to make it, understand?"

"Yes," she mumbled, her reply quavery with emotion.

"Listen, I want you to think about two things."

"Okay."

"First, I want to quit my job." Not until he said the vords did Matt recognize how right it was to leave MicroChip. He should have known it when he was passed ver for a promotion he'd earned. Being undervalued and underappreciated had cut into his self-confidence, and in-vitably, his dissatisfaction with his job had affected his amily life. He couldn't, wouldn't, allow that to continue.

"Quit your job?" Pam gasped.

"It isn't as bad as it sounds. I'm going to send out a couple of feelers right after New Year's. I've got a good eputation in the industry. I can get something else. The nain thing is that I spend more time at home with you and he kids. It's unfair to have you chained down with all the responsibility for them and the house while I travel. I'm going to be looking for a sales position that won't take me away for more than a day at a time.''

''That sounds wonderful.''

''The other thing we need is a vacation, just the two of us. I've got vacation time coming, and it's been far too long since you and I got away without the kids.''

''I'd love that, Matt, more than anything.''

''How about a Caribbean cruise?'' he suggested.

''Yes… Oh, Matt, I love you so much and I've felt so awful about the way our marriage has been going.''

''Me, too. We'll talk about that some more. Maybe it wouldn't be such a bad idea to see a counselor, either.''

''Yes,'' she whispered.

Over the phone Matt heard a chorus of background shouts.

''Your parents just arrived,'' Pam told him.

''Let them wait. I want to say Merry Christmas to my wife.''

# Eight

*"Silent Night"*

Cathy made up a small bed for herself using the blankets and pillows the VFW Women's Auxiliary had distributed. By all rights, she should be exhausted. She'd been up since dawn and the day had been filled with uncertainty and tension.

Instead, she lay with her eyes wide-open, mulling over the events of the past twenty-four hours. Apparently she wasn't the only one having difficulty sleeping. Matt, the sales rep, had carefully made his way across the darkened room and used the phone. It could be her imagination, but his steps seemed lighter on the return trip, as though his mood had improved. Cathy felt pleased for him. She'd lost patience with him earlier, and later…well, later, he'd proved to be an ally and a friend.

She'd witnessed more than one transformation today. The young sailor had been nervous and excited about this trip home; he'd chattered like a five-year-old when they'd first started out.

Then troubles developed, and he'd withdrawn into himself. But over the next few hours, Cathy had watched as Len recovered from his disappointment and frustration. Before the night was over he'd been an encouragement to others.

Nick and Kelly, the young couple with the newborn, were struggling to be good parents and still hold on to the closeness they'd once had in their marriage. Those two reminded Cathy of Ron and her about thirty years ago, after the birth of their first daughter. Eventually, like most couples, Nick and Kelly would learn to work together and ease gracefully into parenthood.

Sam and Louise had kept to themselves all day, offering no advice and little comment until Cathy shared her shortbread cookies. It was then that they'd kindly come forward and contributed their oranges. Later Sam had read the Christmas story from the Bible in a way that had stirred her beyond any Christmas Eve church service she'd ever attended.

She thought again of Matt McHugh. In the beginning he'd been quite disagreeable. Easily irritated, his few remarks cynical. One would assume that as a seasoned traveler he'd be better able to deal with frustrations of this sort. Unfortunately that wasn't the case until… Cathy couldn't put her finger on the precise moment she'd noticed the change in him. About the time they'd decorated the tree, she decided, when he'd opened his briefcase and started folding and clipping memos into paper snowflakes. She'd sensed a genuine enthusiasm in him from that point on.

Cathy had been just as affected by the unusual events of this Christmas Eve as her fellow passengers. That morning, when she'd phoned for a taxi in the middle of the snow-storm, she hadn't been looking forward to the trip. She'd dreaded it less, however, than spending the holiday alone in the house where she'd lived all those years with Ron.

She'd known Christmas would be difficult. After living first with the approach of death and then the aftermath of it, she'd anticipated nothing but pain and loneliness during the Christmas season. And she'd been right. But today, for the first time since standing over her husband's grave, she'd experienced what it meant to be alive. Sharing, encouraging, laughing. Damn, but it felt good.

"Are you awake?" Matt whispered from the bench directly across from her.

"Yes. You, too." She smiled at the obviousness of the comment.

"I just spoke to my wife." He sounded excited. "It was the first time we've connected all day."

"I imagine she was relieved to hear from you."

She saw his nod, and then he said the oddest thing.

"You loved your husband very much, didn't you?" he asked, sitting up and leaning toward her, bracing his elbows on his knees.

"Yes." Her voice wavered slightly, surprised as she was by his question and the instant flash of pain it produced.

"I want my wife and me to have the same kind of relationship you did with your husband."

The comment touched her heart. "Thank you," she whispered, warmed by the praise of this stranger who'd become her friend. "How'd you know... I didn't mention Ron, I don't think."

"Ah, but you did," he said quietly, nestling against his pillow. "You told Kate about the dollhouse your husband built for his granddaughters. It was easy to read between the lines and…well, I could see this Christmas was difficult for you.''

''It's better now,'' she whispered.

He sighed and curled up against the pillow before closing his eyes. ''It's better for me, too.''

''Merry Christmas, Matt.''

''Merry Christmas, Cathy.''

Len purposely waited until the depot was silent. The even rhythm of breathing told him that almost everyone was asleep. His watch said eleven-thirty, which made it ten-thirty in Rawhide. Amy had mentioned playing the piano at the rest home, and he'd waited until he was fairly confident she'd be home.

The phone card he'd paid for on base had long since expired, so he had to use his credit card. The transaction seemed loud enough to wake the entire room, but as far as Len could see, no one stirred.

When the line connected, the phone rang three times, three of the longest rings Len could ever remember hearing. He was about to give up hope when Amy answered.

''Hello.'' Her voice sounded breathless and excited at once.

''Merry Christmas, Amy,'' he said, speaking in a whisper for fear of disturbing the others.

''Len, Len, is that you?''

''It's me.''

''Where are you?''

''The train depot,'' he said, wishing he had other news to give her.

''Still? Oh, Len, are you ever going to make it home?''

''And miss seeing my girl? Are you nuts? I'll walk from here to Rawhide if I have to.''

''Oh, Len! I can't believe this is happening.''

He'd felt much the same way himself most of the day, but somehow everything had changed after Mr. Kemper brought in the Christmas tree. And after the choir had come and the ladies had brought them a meal. And Sam had read the Christmas story…

In the beginning tempers had flared and folks were impatient and short with each other. Then the kindhearted stationmaster had brought that bare sad-looking tree and placed it in the center of the room.

Someone had commented that the stupid tree wasn't worth the buck Kemper had paid for it.

Len had agreed. It'd taken a five-year-old child to teach them. The minute Kate had placed her hair bow on one sagging limb, the Christmas tree had been magically transformed into something beautiful. Not because of what they'd used to decorate its branches, but because of the effect it'd had on all of them, the way it had brought them together.

Everything had changed from then on. Suddenly they weren't strangers anymore. Suddenly it was a Christmas like those he'd enjoyed when he was a boy. He'd spent Christmas Eve with strangers who'd become so much more. Strangers who'd become family. Granted, it wasn't the same as if he'd spent Christmas Eve with Amy, but then he expected to be with her for the rest of his life.

"I'll be home before you know it," he promised.

"I'll be here," she whispered.

The line was quiet a moment while Len gathered his courage. He'd rather propose when he could look into her eyes and see her reaction as he said the words, but that wasn't possible. He didn't think he could wait any longer.

"Did you mean what you said earlier?" he asked. "Do you really love me, Amy Sue?"

"Yes," she admitted as though confessing to a fault. "I…I probably shouldn't have said it."

"Why not?" he asked, raising his voice before he could stop himself.

"Because…well, because we've never talked about our feelings and—"

"I love you, too, Amy."

She didn't say anything for so long Len feared they'd been disconnected.

"Amy?"

"I'm here."

He could tell from the tremble in her voice that she was close to tears. "Amy, listen, I never intended it to happen like this, but then life doesn't always go the way we plan it. I decided to come home for another reason besides spending Christmas with my family."

"What?"

"I was hoping…" Despite rehearsing his proposal, he was tongue-tied and nervous.

"You were hoping…" she encouraged.

"To talk to you about something important."

"Yes?"

"About the two of us." He continued to improvise, forgetting the carefully worded proposal he'd practiced a hundred times. "I was thinking you and I…that is, if you were interested…that maybe we should get married."

There was a silence that seemed to go on and on.

"Married," she finally repeated, sounding stunned.

Len's hand tightened around the telephone receiver. His nerves were stretched to the limit. "Say something," he pleaded, all the while wondering if it was possible to get a refund on the diamond if she refused him. His heart sank to his knees; he hadn't considered Amy's refusal. In his arrogance he'd assumed she'd scream with delight, maybe even cry a little. The last thing he'd anticipated was no response.

"Amy?" he asked, humble now, wondering how he could have made such a mistake in judgment. He'd noted the reserve in her recently, the fact that he hadn't gotten a letter in almost two weeks. Other things didn't add up, either, but he'd pushed his concerns aside each time he spoke with her—although of course their phone calls had been less frequent lately. But whenever he managed to call she'd always sounded so glad to hear from him.

"Is there someone else?" he demanded, his pride rescuing him. "Is that it?"

"Oh, Len, how can you think such a thing?"

"Then what's it to be?" A proposal was a straightforward enough question. "Yes or no?"

"Who told you?"

"Told me?" he echoed. "Told me what?"

"About the baby."

# *Nine*

*"Home For the Holidays"*

"**B**aby?" Len's knees went weak and to remain upright he braced his shoulder against the wall.

"Who told you?" Amy repeated.

"No one..." Len's thoughts twisted around in his mind until he was convinced he'd misunderstood her. "To make sure I understand what's happening here, I need to ask you something. Are you telling me you're pregnant?"

"Yes."

"Don't you think you should've mentioned this before now?" he demanded, not caring who heard him. "You must be at least three months along."

"Three and a half... I love you, Len, but you've never said how you felt about me. I didn't want you to feel obligated to marry me. My dad married my mother because she was pregnant and the marriage was a disaster. I refuse to repeat my mother's mistakes, although I certainly seem to have started out on the same path."

"Amy, listen, I swear I didn't know about the baby. No one told me a damn thing." He took a deep breath. "As for you being like your mom...this is different. I love you. I want us to get married. I wanted it even before I knew about the baby." It hurt to think Amy had held back, not telling him she was pregnant. "Who else knows?"

"Jenny."

"You'd tell your best friend before you'd tell me?" he said, hardly able to believe his ears.

"Why'd you ask me to marry you?" she returned, equally insistent. "Is it just because of the baby?"

"No... I already told you that. Isn't loving you and wanting to spend the rest of my life with you reason enough?"

"Yes," she whispered, whimpering now. "It's more than enough."

"Listen, Amy. I want to be with you. And I want my baby. We're getting married, understand? Soon, too, next week if it can be arranged, and when I go back to Maine, I'm going to ask for married housing. Next month I'll come down and get you."

"Len..."

That was the reason she'd asked if she was just "his girl in Rawhide." He hated the thought of her worrying and fretting all these weeks, wondering how he'd react once he learned the truth.

"You said you love me. Are you taking that back now?" he asked.

"No..."

"I love you. I knew it after my last visit home. I should have said something then. I regret now that I didn't." Then, remembering how he didn't enjoy having his life dictated to him, he asked again, "Will you marry me, Amy?"

Her hesitation was only momentary this time. "Yes, Len, oh, yes."

He could hear her sob softly in the background.

"I knew tonight would be special," she murmured.

"How's that?" Len's mind continued to spin with Amy's news, but it wasn't unwelcome. He was ready to be a husband and had always loved children. His own parents had been wonderful and he was determined to be a good husband and father himself.

"Mr. Danbar came out of his room tonight when I sat down at the piano," Amy told him.

Len could only vaguely recall the man's name. "Mr. Danbar?"

"He's the one who hasn't spoken a word since his wife died three years ago. The man I eat my lunch with every day. I'm the one who does all the talking, but that's all right."

"He came out of his room?" This was big news, Len realized. He remembered now that Amy had written to him about the older gentleman.

"His wife used to play the piano and when he heard the music, he climbed out of bed and came into the recreation room. He sat down on the bench beside me and smiled. Oh, Len, it was the most amazing thing."

His wife-to-be was pretty darn amazing herself, he thought proudly. She could coax a lonely old man from his room and brighten his life with her music and kindness. Len meant what he'd said, about their marrying as soon as possible. Their marriage would be a strong one, based on love and mutual respect.

He felt like the luckiest man alive.

"Are you awake?" Nick whispered to Kelly in the dead of night. He thought he'd heard her stir and realized they were both accustomed to Brittany waking and needing to be fed around this time.

Nick had been wide-awake for the better part of an hour. Sleeping upright with his head propped against the wall had been awkward, but he'd managed to get some rest. It helped to have his arm around Kelly and hold her close to his side. They hadn't held each other nearly enough lately, but that was something he hoped to remedy.

In response to his question, Kelly yawned. "What time is it?"

"About two."

"Already?" His wife smothered a second yawn. "How's Brittany?"

"Better than either of us."

Nick grinned into the darkness and gently squeezed her shoulder.

"I never thought we'd spend our first Christmas as parents stuck in some train depot," Kelly said, her words barely audible.

"Me, neither."

"It hasn't been so bad."

Nick pressed his face into her hair and inhaled, delighting in her warm female scent. He loved Kelly and Brittany more than he'd thought it was possible to love anyone. More than it seemed reasonable for any human heart to love. Little in his life had come easy, and this parenting business might well be his greatest challenge yet. But his struggles had taught him to appreciate what he did have. Tonight, Christmas Eve, had taught him to *recognize* what he had.

He'd considered the trip home to Georgia unnecessary, but Kelly had wanted to introduce Brittany to her grandparents. Besides, traveling in winter was a mistake, he'd told her over and over. In the end he'd agreed only because Kelly had wanted it so badly. He hadn't been gracious about it, and when troubles arose, it was all he could do not to leap up and tell her how right he'd been.

Nick felt differently now. Being with these people on Christmas Eve hadn't been a mistake at all. Nor was taking Brittany to meet her extended family. They needed each other. He'd stood alone most of his life, but he wasn't alone anymore. He had a wife and daughter. Family. And friends.

More friends than he'd realized.

At six o'clock Christmas morning, Clayton Kemper received word that the tracks had been repaired. He hurriedly dressed and rushed down to the train depot, not sure what he'd find. It came as a pleasant surprise to discover everyone waking up in a good mood, grateful to hear his news. While the travelers stretched and yawned, Clayton put on a pot of coffee, then dragged out the phone book and called the hotels in town to alert the passengers there that the tracks had been repaired.

"I don't imagine this will be a Christmas you'll soon forget," Clayton said as he led the small band from the depot to the train. The engine hummed, ready to race down the tracks toward Boston.

Mrs. Norris was the first to board. She smiled as she placed her hand in his. "Thank you again for all your kindness, Mr. Kemper. And Merry Christmas."

"I was glad I could help," he said as she climbed onto the train.

The couple with the baby followed, along with the young navy man who lugged his own bag as well as the infant seat. It never ceased to amaze Clayton that one baby could need this much equipment. Time was, a bottle or two and a few diapers would suffice. These days it took the mother and two full-grown men to cart everything in. Clayton was pleased to see that the couple had struck up a friendship with the sailor. They certainly seemed to have a great deal to talk about.

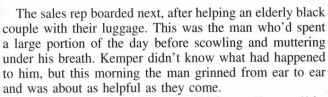 

The sales rep boarded next, after helping an elderly black couple with their luggage. This was the man who'd spent a large portion of the day before scowling and muttering under his breath. Kemper didn't know what had happened to him, but this morning the man grinned from ear to ear and was about as helpful as they come.

"We appreciate everything you did for us, Kemper," he said as he made his way into the train.

Five-year-old Kate bounced onto the first step and told Clayton, "Santa came last night and dropped off a present for me and Charles."

"Did he now?" Clayton asked, catching Elise Jones's eyes.

"Indeed he did," Elise said with a wide smile.

Apparently the adults had arranged something for the children. Clayton was glad to hear it. He wished he'd been able to do more himself, but he had his own family and plenty of obligations. It was a sad case when the railroad had to put people up in a depot for the night, especially when that night happened to be Christmas Eve.

He waited until everyone was on board before he stepped away from the train. Glancing inside the compartment, he watched fascinated as the group of once-cantankerous travelers cheerfully teased one another. Anyone looking at them would assume they were lifelong friends, even family.

Was it possible, Clayton wondered, that this small band of strangers had discovered the true meaning of Christmas? Learned it in a train depot late on Christmas Eve in the middle of a snowstorm?

The question seemed to answer itself.